THE GARDENS
OF EDEN
LIFE AND TIMES OF ADAM AND EVE

Richard E. Warren

ISBN: 9781707553655

ABOUT THE AUTHOR

Richard "Rick" Warren is a father, a grandfather, a thirty-year student of *The Urantia Book*, and a writer of Urantia-based novels. "The Gardens Of Eden" is his third book, after "Resurrection Hall," and "Battlefield Guardians."

Editor-in-chief, Story Consultant: James Woodward
Contributing Editor: Suzanne M. Kelly

Formatting: Rick Lyon
Cover design: Susan Lyon
CosmicCreations.BIZ

Cover art: Holly Carmichael

Original cover art, "Fantasy Garden" by Holly Carmichael of Antioch, TN, USA.
https://holly-carmichael.pixels.com/

Artist's Concept of the First Garden of Eden

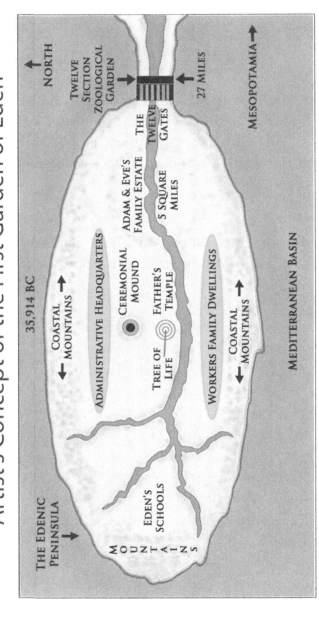

THE EDENIC PENINSULA

35,914 BC

NORTH

TWELVE SECTION ZOOLOGICAL GARDEN

27 MILES

MESOPOTAMIA

THE TWELVE GATES

ADAM & EVE'S FAMILY ESTATE

5 SQUARE MILES

COASTAL MOUNTAINS

ADMINISTRATIVE HEADQUARTERS

CEREMONIAL MOUND

FATHER'S TEMPLE

TREE OF LIFE

WORKERS FAMILY DWELLINGS

COASTAL MOUNTAINS

MEDITERRANEAN BASIN

EDEN'S SCHOOLS

MOUNTAINS

° CAPACITY: 1,000,000
° 12,000 + MILES OF ROADWAYS
° THOUSANDS OF MILES OF IRRIGATION DITCHES

° 5,000 BRICK BUILDINGS
° LARGEST HOUSING CLUSTER = 7
° 20% UNDER CULTIVATION WHEN ADAM & EVE ARRIVE

Location of the Second Garden of Eden

CASPIAN SEA

ZAGROS MOUNTAINS

56 MILE WALL

TIGRIS

MESOPOTAMIA

EUPHRATES

FATHER'S TEMPLE

SECOND GARDEN

250 MILES

DEAD SEA

FIRST GARDEN

MEDITERRANEAN BASIN

The Gardens Of Eden

Dedicated to William and Lena Sadler

Tables Of Contents

Chapter   TITLE

The Gardens Of Eden

X

Chapter 1

IN THE BEGINNING

This story has been in our family for 1,501 generations. My long-ago grandmother, known only by her first name, Lyla, started the tradition of reciting it every year at family reunions.

Lyla and her mate, Lam, were Adam and Eve's original, personal aides. And they were parents to fourteen children and innumerable grandchildren. Each generation chose from their ranks, one who would, reliably and responsibly, bear the title: "Lyla, Keeper of the Story."

The alternate story keeper, in case of the death or disability of the presiding Lyla, was given the title-name Lam, in honor of Lyla's original mate. After the first few generations, there were always several sets of Lylas and Lams alive at once. But only the most recently elected pair was the official Keeper. The emeritus members served in an advisory capacity regarding translation and preservation, and in emergencies that threatened the story's continuity.

It was the original Lyla's life-long duty, on Adam's request, to maintain and pass on an accurate history of Adam and Eve's life and times "for the benefit of far-away generations." But, I am the last Lyla, and this written account is to ensure that all coming generations will not be deprived of this remarkable story when I die.

Because of circumstances beyond anyone's foresight, including falling birth-rates, the global dispersion of my family, and sagging interest in what many count as religious fairy tales—I have become the final Lyla, the last one who knows the entire story just as it was passed down. Scattered family

1

members know parts of it, but only I recall the whole story, beginning to end.

Our family's service as personal aides went unbroken during the long lives of Adam and Eve, and then continued uninterrupted, serving their children and grandchildren. Down the generations the story flowed, from one Lyla to the next. Additions were made only when they involved the Adamic bestowal's direct or residual effects on the evolution of civilization.

Adam and Eve arrived on Earth 37,933 years ago (from 2019) and lived for 530, and 511 years, respectively. After their deaths we descendants of the original Lyla (who lived 102 years) went on serving the Adamic family. Each Lyla kept the story safe and alive, preserving the facts and details. And it wasn't always easy, keeping such a detailed story both accurate and intact across so many millennia, over so many oceans, and translated through so many languages.

We are fortunate the former Lylas wholly dedicated themselves to it. Because of their efforts this story can now be broadcast over the emerging global network, to a great many sincere truth-seekers simultaneously. Those earnestly searching for the facts of our origin, a record of our lost history, and some certainty of a desirable destiny—both personal and planetary—can now find it.

Everyone connected to the family, by marriage or friendship, was invited to our yearly reunions. As many as two hundred attended when I was a child, nine decades ago. Aside from hearing the story of the Gardens, they came because these familial conclaves were always enjoyable, fulfilling, and life-affirming.

Year after year we gathered at the same country retreat for a week enjoying each other's company, playing music, singing, dancing, and feasting. But when evening came a certain nostalgic reverence drew us together to hear the old stories, always presented by the presiding Lyla, or one of her surrogates. The story was told in seven parts, one each night of reunion week.

But, gradually, during my lifetime, the family scattered around the globe and participation declined rather rapidly. It is now at a point that we few remaining family members decided a record should be published so that the story would not perish with us.

It is regrettable that I am forced to commit to paper what a gifted story-keeper would present so much better in person. In narrating this story by printed text, I did in every way possible attempt to portray the scenes and the dialog as they were so vividly described during our annual, live, oral presentations.

Lyla 1501, August 21, 2019

Chapter 2

ARRIVAL OF ADAM & EVE

"Welcome!" shouted Van from the center of the courtyard of the Father's Temple. He looked out on the assembled crowd and said in strong voice, "When a world is ready our Creator Father sends forth a Son and a Daughter, ones who have been specially trained and duly selected for service on such worlds.

"Let us rejoice that the Earth may, on this very day, welcome our Son and Daughter, visible beings who have volunteered for this mission to raise *all* the children of the Earth to new heights. This world has not been forgotten, nor have we been abandoned. The Great Father knows all, and wisely provides for all, even for the least of his God-knowing creatures.

"Again, I say, welcome Adam, and welcome Eve, as the Earth's new leaders, enlightened teachers, and personal friends!"

When the cheering ceased, two children standing behind Van pulled open a circular veil and out stepped a tall female and an equally tall male. Both were magnificent beings, divinely handsome, and perfect in proportion. Their most striking feature was slightly glowing violet skin. The throng was stunned silent at first. Some couldn't believe their eyes, others dropped to their knees in reverence.

The temple courtyard overflowed with Garden residents and guests. Most were standing or perched on its low walls. The beautiful couple scanned their audience, many of whom had for generations been hearing about and anticipating this momentous occasion. Eve and Adam's initial reaction on seeing their enthusiastic welcomers with mouths and eyes agape, was a heavenly captivating smile.

As the people and the pair continued to scan the other, a tremendous roaring cheer broke out, echoing off the courtyard's walls and up to the open sky. Everyone in the Garden, and most in the nearby villages, knew Adam and Eve had arrived ten days before. On this day the pair achieved full consciousness and were properly greeted by these wildly cheering Garden residents and guests.

A series of large and small caravans had been travelling to the Garden hoping to arrive in time for the official welcoming ceremony. Hundreds of guests were present that day in the temple's courtyard, amid almost three thousand Garden volunteers and their families. And everyone was delighted to be able to participate in this grand welcome. The moment had finally arrived, and everyone beamed at the miraculous event they were witnessing.

Van said this when the cheering waned, "When Adam and Eve arrived, after the long voyage to this world, I informed you it would require ten days to prepare their new material life forms. These unique bodies were designed and created by the Life Carriers, an order of beings whose work it is to do such remarkable things. They are also responsible for designing and planting life on the Earth. In time, over millions of years, these life seeds sprout, flower, then bear their intended fruit, human life such as yours.

"But they may and do create bodies in a matter of days, such as mine, and Eve's, and Adam's. Look but you will not see the Life Carriers. However, you can see their personalized creations standing before you!" Eve and Adam were smiling radiantly. They bowed slightly, which was followed by the loudest cheers yet.

Curiosity, rumor, and speculation had swirled endlessly, about this materialization process that required ten days, resulting in the creation of the bodies of Adam and Eve. Their bodies were designed to live on forever when their diet is regularly supplemented with the fruit of the Tree of Life.

These citizens of the Garden knew that Van, and his companion, Amadon, had lived on Earth for thousands of years, replenished by that Tree of Life. And all Garden workers had been informed this tree would likewise sustain the specially constructed physical forms of Adam and Eve.

Van and Amadon had arranged a private reception when Adam and Eve arrived by seraphic transport ten days previously. The essence of the pair was suspended in a special chamber of the Father's Temple while the Life Carriers created physical forms perfectly suited for habitation on Earth. Van and Amadon alone attended this period of incarnation and adjustment.

Before the arrival of Adam and Eve, Van taught that, "For most beings, seraphic transport is the only method available for travel from one world to another. When the transporting angels bring an Adam and an Eve to their assigned world, new bodies, specially designed for that environment, are always provided.

"The bodies of our Adam and Eve are blood and bone, like yours. But they are also fed by an unseen source of life energy that flows throughout the universe; it is of spirit origin. That cosmic force, along with the fruit of the Tree of Life, will keep Adam and Eve alive without decay, just as they have kept Amadon and me alive and well for many ages. Humans have not the capacity for this ministry. Your bodies will die ere long. But take heart! After death you will resume life in resurrected form on the mansion worlds. And from those mansions you will continue in the pursuit of truth and perfection, even into eternity."

Van also taught his human associates that 162,000 years before Adam and Eve came, he and Amadon became stewards of the Tree of Life. When the planetary rebellion broke out, they became its sole custodians. Van and Amadon's bodies were sustained all those millennia by the tree and the spirit energy it absorbs from surrounding space. This plant, when just a shrub, was imported from Edentia, headquarters of the constellation, the sphere whereon the Most Highs abide, and the origin of the name Eden.

The shrub had been delivered to the Earth one-half million years before, with the coming of the previous rulers of the Earth, the Planetary Prince and his staff. It was planted at the center of their temple of the Father. There it grew to become a great tree. But, after 300,000 years, the Prince and many of his staff betrayed their trust and broke their oath to the Most Highs to faithfully minister to the people of Earth.

When full rebellion broke out and the tree was threatened, Van and Amadon departed. They carved out the tree's living core and took it to the safety of the Asian highlands. There they remained for 162,000 years, isolated by rebellion and betrayed by their leaders.

Their vigil ended when humanity had evolved enough physically to warrant a call for the next order of sonship, an Adam and an Eve. Unfortunately, the rebellion wiped out nearly all the intellectual and spiritual advances the Prince and his staff had made during the 300,000 years of his administration, the pre-rebellion years. This betrayal of trust by superhuman leaders had little to no effect on biological progress. Humanity continued its gradual physical advancement throughout, reaching its peak about the same time the pair arrived.

It was in the mountains of Asia that Van and Amadon watched and waited, all the while anticipating the arrival of an angelic committee to pronounce the Earth ready for an Adam and Eve, and one to scout a suitable and secure location for their Garden. Van knew that was the next step in Earth's evolution. He long predicted the coming of these committees, followed by Adam and Eve.

The approval committee visited one hundred years before Adam and Eve arrived. Van was informed that its leader, one named Tabamantia, had decided the Earth was indeed ready for the next order of sonship.

The location committee, after a three-year tour of the Earth, decided on three sites. The best of the three was in southwest Asia. When this location was approved by the planetary supervisors, Van and Amadon left their highland retreat. They packed all things needed, including the core of the Tree of Life, and traveled to a long, wide peninsula jutting westward off the eastern shores of the Mediterranean Basin. There it was replanted in what became the central courtyard of the Father's Temple.

During the seventeen years that followed the location committee's report, Van and Amadon began gathering and transporting all the materials needed. They also started selecting the workers who would be needed to prepare the peninsula for Adam and Eve's imminent arrival.

Once things were in place, the Tree of Life was in the soil, and the first work crews had been assembled, Van started a school. He taught the workers and their families about his, and the Earth's, unusual history.

"Unlike you, I had life before coming to the Earth. But I began like you, as a babe of the realm, long, long ago, on another world not far distant.

"When the Earth was ripe, one hundred former mortals, like myself, were brought here as part of the first planetary administration. We were personalized in the form you see now, as Adam and Eve will be when they arrive.

"My human associate, Amadon, was, like all humans, born of a woman. But the Life Carriers transformed his body. They realigned and attuned his body to the life-giving properties of the Tree of Life. In fact, such bodies as ours, and the bodies that Eve and Adam will receive, are designed to endure as long as needed. Tens of thousands, even hundreds of thousands, of years may be required for Adam and Eve to achieve their assigned mission. Therefore are their bodies constructed to live on and on, but only with the aid of the special restorative properties of the Tree of Life, which have the ability to gather and make useful certain essential spirit energies."

For more than eighty years Van and Amadon taught the Garden dwellers, simultaneously leading them in the preparations, the clearing, planting, and landscaping.

Van's predictions of Adam and Eve's coming finally materialized on this auspicious day. Here stood these two radiant beings in their newly created, strikingly beautiful and statuesque bodies. Van turned to his ever-faithful aide Amadon, and commanded with blissful finality, "Send forth the message to our friends abroad, Adam and Eve have arrived! Release the birds!"

Amadon gave a silent signal and two runners hastened to the nearby aviary. Caged there were hundreds of carrier pigeons who had been gathered and trained for this predicted occasion. The runners yelled out to the birds' keepers the words they had so long wished to deliver, "Let loose the birds! Let the word go out, the promised ones are here!"

When this official message was received on wing by the surrounding villages, many were confirmed in what they had heard and hoped for regarding the expected Son and Daughter. No longer was it a rumor. The new world leaders, reportedly sent by ones having God's authority, had finally arrived, alive for all to see, hear, and engage.

On receiving this message plans were laid by many once-doubting local villagers, for immediate pilgrimages to Eden. Not long thereafter, selected delegations from each village marched to one of Eden's twelve gates, there to seek entrance, then to see and hear for themselves this celestial couple.

These delegations returned and reported their findings to families and village elders. After that, almost all village councils began making plans for their people, young and old, male and female, to visit Eden. Nearly all felt privileged to live near such a place as now hosts these two divine visitors. But there were a few leaders who reacted in fear, boldly declaring Adam and Eve were alien invaders and that, "They should be destroyed."

Meanwhile, the welcoming ceremony was well underway. Van invited the pair to address their new subjects. They stepped forward, looking over the adoring crowd. All fell silent. Then, in perfect dialect of the Garden (as taught by Van and Amadon, and fully mastered by Eve and Adam before coming to Earth), the two said in resonate voice and perfect harmony, "Greetings friends," bowing slightly and gazing out on their new family of Garden builders.

Shouts of hearty welcome came from this awestruck and astounded group of mortals. Adam and Eve searched their faces, noting the joy, enthusiasm, and sincerity. They then bestowed on their admirers another god-like smile. The cheering response immediately endeared Adam and Eve to these humble and earnest souls who had worked hard, and waited patiently, to meet the world's promised heavenly-appointed leaders.

The sounds of cheering could be heard far from this holy place. The few workers, children, and Garden guests in the area who weren't already at the central temple turned and ran toward it yelling out, "They are here!"

Amid the raucous cheers Lyla and Lam exchanged glances of incredulous amazement and barely contained glee, ecstatic in the knowledge that they alone had been selected as aides to these divine beings. This was a long moment of uninterrupted adulation before Adam raised a hand to draw the audience's attention. He and Eve wished to show proper appreciation for this enthusiastic welcome.

As the cheering subsided, Adam spoke these few but deeply felt words, "Eve and I have come to serve. We are grateful for this warm and joyous welcome." The lovely pair looked out on their adoring subjects, already sensing a mutual affection.

Then Eve spoke, "Adam and I want you to know our sole desire is to serve this world as our Father would have it. We came to fulfill the mission given us by the Most Highs and sanctioned by the Father of All." Another long round of applause broke out. It did not escape the attention of the group that Eve spoke with the same authority and clarity, the same impressive bearing, confidence, and ease, as did Adam.

Van stepped in front of the pair. Amadon moved to his side. The two led Adam and Eve through an opening in the temple's circular altar and down three steps to its center aisle. As the foursome moved forward, the crowd parted, making a narrow path to the main entry.

Van and Amadon led the procession out of the temple and onto a broad and beautifully landscaped path that led to a specially prepared ceremonial mount just north of the Father's Temple. This mount was in fact a natural hill that had been built up and artfully sculpted for the pair's reception and inauguration.

As the celestial pair walked with Van and Amadon toward the elevated site, the ever-growing throng of enthralled residents and guests followed close behind, now laughing and dancing. No solemn moment was this!

Walking unhurriedly, Adam and Eve paused a moment for a first long look at the Garden's expanse. They noted its long, broad valley in the center of a ring of high hills that were situated in front of mountain ranges. Peering over the heads of the group, they immediately recognized the vast potential for rearing family and raising food. The Garden was at its peak season when they arrived.

Even in its early years Eden was the most beautiful place on all the Earth, botanically speaking, thanks mostly to its luxuriant subtropical locale. It soon became much more so as a result of the foresight, planning, and sweat-labor Van, Amadon, and their loyal followers put forth.

Even so, when Adam and Eve arrived, they had only begun to build Eden. But the pair, right then and there on the path to the inaugural mount, envisioned their goal of one-half-million pure line children to carry the Adamic blood and ideals to the entire world. And that would be but the first phase of their long, long ministry, beginning as biologic-uplifters and teachers of truth, ending as world leaders and glorified ministers, accredited representatives of God on Earth.

Before their arrival, Van taught that Adamic pairs were intended to be the Universal Father's visible and authoritative representatives, ones who will spend many millennia preparing Earth for the next order of ministering Sons of God. By the original plan, Adam and Eve were expected to remain on Earth 100,000 years or more, eventually to inaugurate the next phase of planetary progress and enlightenment, the dawning of the ages of "Light and Life."

As they resumed this short walk to the ceremonial mount, striding slowly and obviously enjoying themselves, more workers and guests arrived. They lined the pathway ahead or fell in behind with the jubilance-makers. Everyone commented on the pair's breath-taking beauty, unusual skin tone, dignified demeanor, and perfect poise. Many along the path dared not look upon Adam and Eve's magnificent, lightly-clad, violet-skinned bodies. They instead took to their knees and bowed their heads when the pair passed.

As soon as Adam, Eve, Van, and Amadon topped the mount, a group of young helpers, chosen and trained by Amadon, came forward to meet them. As these two groups exchanged greetings, the crowd was forming a ring below, standing or sitting on the grassy surface.

All watched as more workers poured into the area, filling out the ring until it extended well beyond the mount's base. With genuine and unaffected dignity Eve and Adam stood high simply observing and taking in this memorable moment.

After settling, Amadon signaled for the assembly's attention. He began the ceremony saying: "With humble thanksgiving and tremendous gratitude we of the Earth now welcome our new leaders sent from on high. Adam and Eve are, like us, servants of the Universal Father, the One God of all, and over all. They are our friends and we welcome them in recognition of the wisdom and sovereignty of the Most Highs, those who rule our world in the Father's name. It was the Most Highs who granted Adam and Eve stewardship of this world. We now formally install them as our new leaders."

A huge roar of approval came from the thousands around the mount, many layers deep now. Amadon invited Eve and Adam to "Greet the people of the Earth." They slowly walked a circle around the top of the hill, their beaming smiles endearing everyone present. A wonderful and wordless being-to-being connection occurred in that moment. It was the beginning of a long and loving association between Garden dwellers and their new Garden administrators.

After walking a full circle, they stopped and Amadon gave a signal to his helpers. Adam and Eve were approached from behind by four youngsters who were there to bestow a gift from the people. The two couples were each carrying a magnificent robe. These regal robes, crafted by Garden volunteers, were unfolded and made ready to adorn the honorees.

The diminutive couples stood on their toes attempting to lift the robes over Eve and Adam's high shoulders. The gracious pair bent humbly to assist them. Still, the little ones stretched to place the beautifully woven capes on the pair. A gentle laugh wafted over the throng as they watched the earnest children who, with that kindly assist from Adam and Eve, accomplished their task.

Then the oath was administered by Van. He stepped forward and said in commanding voice, "Adam and Eve, number 14,311 of your order, presently assigned to the biological, cultural, and spiritual uplift of this isolated and quarantined planet, do you now and forever pledge loyalty, fidelity, and allegiance to God the Father, to Michael of Nebadon—creator of the local universe of ten million planets— to the Most Highs and Constellation Fathers of Edentia, and to the Melchizedek Council of Overseers? And do you now pledge your lives to the service and uplift of the mortal children of this world until the Most Highs bid you return to Jerusem?"

Eve and Adam affirmed the pledges, saying simply, "We do." Van then turned to the Garden laborers and managers saying, "Let this world, and this Garden that you have labored so long to prepare, now come under the beneficent ministry and wise guidance of Adam and Eve." Turning back to the pair, he added, "Divine speed in your mission, as our Father leads you." Another great roar of approval burst out.

The time had come for Van to relinquish his title as temporary leader, even the hero of a world devastated by rebellion. He looked to the pair and said with genuine solemnity, "To you Adam, and to you Eve, are given this day, the title and direction of the affairs of the Earth. With the authority of the Most Highs and the consent of the Council of Melchizedek Receivers, I now proclaim you Earth's rulers. May you serve it well, with wisdom and foresight. And may those who you rule be ever faithful, true, and loyal, in every way consistent with your mission. We pray to the Universal Father for great success on this darkened world, that cooperation and harmony dominate the hearts and minds of all as you carry out your mission to uplift and enlighten the peoples of Earth."

Now, quite surprisingly to the thousands in attendance, Adam, Eve, Van, and Amadon appeared to hear and see something. Their attention was obviously being drawn to some invisible event. What the four heard was Gabriel's call for the resurrection of the sleeping survivors of the previous epoch. The new Adamic dispensation was this day established and inaugurated, under the superhuman leadership of Adam and Eve.

Every worker and visitor felt a chill of astonishment and joy as they observed the four in rapt attention, even though they saw and heard nothing. After a short while, Van broke the tension, saying to the assembly, "Unseen by you, Archangels are in our midst. Millions of slumbering souls have been ushered off to the resurrection halls of the system's mansion worlds, there to receive new life and new bodies of a spiritual nature. All those resurrected mortals will now continue the heavenly journey wherefrom Adam and Eve have so recently descended. And where you will ascend after your last breath."

Then he added, "It has been ten days since the angelic transporters brought Adam and Eve to the planet. Know you now, that on this day, and in the presence of the Melchizedek Receivers, the Earth's newest leaders are hereby granted custody and direction of planetary affairs."

Van went on, asking rhetorically, "Who are Adam and Eve? They are the offspring of the original pair of that order. They were born, much as you were, and they are reared on the capital sphere of our local system, a world named Jerusem.

"After maturing, and after extensive training, Adams and Eves may be selected and assigned to an evolving world, of which there are many. Their mission is always up-lift, improving the bodies and minds, and consequently the entire civilizations, of the worlds of their assignment.

"Before coming to the Earth, our Adam and Eve served together, in fact, for many thousands of years. Previously, they worked as co-administrators of the life laboratories on Jerusem. And before that they were teachers in the system's citizenship schools. When the Earth was ready for the next stage of its biologic and cultural advancement, a call for volunteers went out. The entire senior corps of Adam and Eves responded affirmatively. Eventually these two were chosen.

"All those born into the Order of Material Sons and Daughters are service-minded celestial citizens who also, on occasion, volunteer for incarnation duty on evolutionary planets like Earth. Our Adam and Eve descended from their permanent home, Jerusem. This is an advanced world wherefrom the one thousand evolutionary worlds of our system, worlds like the Earth, are administered. Someday *you* will arrive on that capital sphere, their birth home, and become its citizens, as they were before coming to Earth.

"When an Adamic pair is chosen to up-step a mortal planet and succeeds in their mission it greatly accelerates evolution. Our Adam and Eve will create a family of one-half million of their own children and grandchildren. When that distant goal has been achieved, their sons and daughters will begin leaving the Garden, taking its culture to every land, marrying the sons and daughters of the Earth, thereby establishing the dawn of an advanced civilization. In this endeavor, let us pledge unwavering support and loyalty."

Cheers of approval rose to the sky.

Van paused a moment, then looked at the pair saying, "And let us now escort our new administrators on a walk in their Garden."

The regal entourage led the way down the mount to an adjacent botanical park where Eve exclaimed, "Such beauty abounds here. You all are to be congratulated."

Adam smiled at Eve and added, "And already have you begun to think of improvements." Eve laughed and everyone who heard was enchanted by the sound of it.

The Garden tour lasted until long after noon. Adam and Eve marveled at what had already been done to make the Garden habitable, beautiful, and productive. And those following, ones who could hear, were astounded by their knowledge of the properties and potentials of each and every plant.

Finally, Van announced an end to the formal welcome. He stood atop a boulder and addressed the throng, "Go you now. Prepare yourselves for the great celebration and welcoming banquet the day after tomorrow!" Some but not all heeded Van's dismissal.

Chapter 3

FIRST AFTERNOON AND EVENING

With the formal ceremony over, the pair spent the rest of the daylight hours touring the Garden grounds. Passing by, they greeted and thanked many Garden workers and their supervisors. And to the great delight of Garden guests and their children, Adam and Eve stopped to converse casually. Everyone was instantly enamored with them. The women and men they met were immediately charmed by the couples' every word and gesture.

Van and Amadon had interviewed hundreds of couples and finally selected Lyla and Lam to become personal aides to the celestial visitors. Finally, the time came for Van to introduce them. The tour halted as Van asked the couple to step forward. Lyla and Lam felt extremely honored, and humbled, now about to receive a personal greeting from what they felt were visiting gods.

Van introduced them, saying, "Lyla and Lam were chosen from over six hundred couples, Garden residents who volunteered to serve at your home, and by your side, for as long as they shall live. And when their time comes to depart the Earth, their children will have been taught and trained as replacements. Lyla and Lam have pledged to carry out your wishes, plans, and orders. They and their children will serve you and your children for as long as you desire such service.

"Also, Lyla has been informed that you will likely want to maintain an enduring record of the Adamic family's doings and its effect on world culture and history. She and Lam have been trained in the skills required to keep such a record. Without your objection, they will keep it in both oral and written forms. This human record will complement the celestial record and serve to inform the inhabitants of the Earth of their history for generations to come."

Immediately Adam and Eve took their new attendants in light embrace. Both were struck speechless with joy. For years before their arrival, Van had been teaching Lyla, Lam, and other Garden citizens about Adam, Eve, about their life before coming to Earth. He accurately estimated their needs and made certain the pair would have the things, and the assistance, that would be required on, and after, their arrival.

Reading and writing were obligatory courses in all Garden schools, for children and adults. Van attempted to create a reasonably literate group among the Garden's workers before Adam's coming. The language Van taught originated with the first humans. He and Amadon took that simple tongue and expanded it, creating an alphabet having twenty-four characters.

Accordingly, in the years before Adam and Eve came, the schools introduced thousands of new words, innovative ideas, and advanced concepts so that Adam and Eve's work would be easier. In matters of education the Garden was already far above any outside cultures.

By the time the pair arrived there existed this vastly improved written language within the Garden. Before their arrival, angels who had visited Earth carried this improved tongue back to Jerusem where they taught it to Adam and Eve. That, by itself, created an enormous advantage in making a positive first impression.

The Garden was originally staffed and maintained by volunteer families who once resided in villages on the mainland. All were screened for physical and mental fitness, and then brought in for a probationary period under a sponsorship program. These first volunteers and their descendants had labored for four generations to make the peninsula habitable and productive.

Van reported that almost every nearby village had at least one family of volunteers working and residing in the Garden. In the beginning, most volunteers were couples without children. It was decided that young parents-to-be, adaptable laborers and potential administrators, would be selected so that the Adamic culture might be more quickly established in their lives, and most especially in the lives of their Garden-born children.

Almost everyone in the region wished to live and work inside Eden. And there was no shortage of volunteers willing to serve in the home of Eve and Adam, or their children, or anywhere on the Adamic estate. All envied Lyla and Lam's role as personal aides. When Eve and Adam arrived, only one couple was required for that cherished assignment. Eventually, as both families grew, more aides were needed. The original Lyla and Lam, and their descendants, always provided them.

When old enough, Lyla and Lam's children were carefully trained as replacements. This was done by simply observing and assisting their parents and grandparents. This system provided a permanent, trained, and always expanding staff of personal aides for the ever-increasing Adamic family. It also provided abundant assistants to help with the documentation and preservation of their momentous story.

It took many decades and several generations of volunteer planners, Garden workers, and skilled artisans to prepare for this day of reception. There had been hurdles and problems along the way. Early on, some workers left the Garden when Van announced, in complete honesty, that older workers would probably not live long enough to witness the arrival of the promised visitors. "But your children and their children will," he declared. About twenty years before Adam and Eve arrived the first Lyla and Lam were born.

The announced delay caused a wave of desertions. But Lyla's and Lam's parents and grandparents chose to stay. They never lost faith because they believed and trusted Van. Never did Lyla, Lam, or any of their family members ever seriously doubt Van's prediction of a superhuman planetary administration.

The eight decades of preparation for the arrival of Adam and Eve were trying times of valiant struggle and endless toil. Even so, less than a quarter of the Garden was complete when they incarnated. All remaining development would be their task and the many yet-to-be born generations of violet-skinned horticulturists and engineers.

The Garden was in full bloom at the time of their arrival. No place on Earth was more beautiful or had more potential than this long, elevated peninsula with a wide, flat, central valley. Mountains, providing both a secure interior and plentiful rain, surrounded the valley. The rain on these coastal mountains assured that the rivers would always be a reliable source for drinking and irrigation. It did not rain often in the valley, but the heavy morning mists daily fed the Garden's innumerable plants, shrubs, and trees.

Adam taught that the Garden site was selected from three suitable locations. The selection committee, led by the assigned planetary inspector, had visited the Earth a hundred years previously. Of the three favored sites, this peninsula was deemed the most ideal for the garden-estate of Adam and Eve. After hearing the report, Van and Amadon journeyed from their cold mountain home in eastern Asia, where they had upheld the light of civilization and truth for over 160,000 years, and moved onto this perfectly suited peninsula.

The Garden site was a sheltered and safe place from which Eve and Adam's potent progeny could go forth to add the violet race's heritage to that of the planet's indigenous peoples, thereby accomplishing in a relatively brief period what would otherwise require ages of evolution.

But biological conditions have to be ripe before uplifters can be dispatched for the age long work of establishing and maintaining divine order on an evolutionary planet. Finally, that day had arrived. The visible representatives of God once again appeared before the eyes and ears of humans.

Before Adam and Eve's arrival, Van taught, "When they are assigned, it is their solemn duty to create a better world of gardeners. In fact, such bestowal worlds are destined to become global Edens, bearing up not only better foods, but also souls prepared for the greater glories of eternal life, beginning after death and resurrection on the mansion worlds. And the culture they eventually create, over many thousands of years, approaches a true utopian age of Light and Life."

Van once said to Lyla, "The Earth and innumerable planets like it are soul incubators, spirit nurseries. But they are destined to become celestial showcases of the limitless potentials and actual manifestations of divine and human creativity combined. God is a senior partner to man and woman in creation. God, women, and men, need each other.

"The dispersion of the violet culture on a world causes the native inhabitants to develop a keen interest in play, humor, and art. The dominant concern of pre-Adamic mortals is trying to appease imaginary spirits who are believed to be the cause of all their troubles, even a human's final ordeal, death.

"During and after the graft of Adamic culture onto an evolved human culture, that world begins the journey to a higher destiny. Ignorant superstition and ghost fear of the past give way to intelligent prayer and meaningful worship. The Earth is now on a long trek into a glorious future where people do not make war or even die. Rather do they *translate* directly to the mansion worlds when their mortal lives are fulfilled. Despite the tragic retrogressions brought about by mutiny and isolation, planetary progress is inevitable. Earth's culture will grow and flower majestically in the ages to come. The ministry of the descending sons and daughters of God insure that."

The more advanced Garden citizens had been told that Earth was socially, culturally, and spiritually retarded by the rebellion against the government of God (which began during the previous planetary administration, and from which Van and Amadon emerged as loyal heroes).

But physically, Earth's inhabitants were not behind schedule. The Earth was ready for an up-step in biologic endowment, even though progress in invention, leisure, the arts, and commerce all lagged far behind biological development.

One day, before Adam and Eve arrived, Van said this to Lyla in response to her question about the origin and history of the Earth: "About five-hundred million years ago the Life Carriers initiated life on the Earth. They planted a unique life formula in three places, all shallow tidal pools located on seashores. From those life seeds grew a vast diversity of plant and creature forms. Over many millions of years, the Life Carrier implants evolved ever-more-complex living things, and eventually there came into existence human bodies with human minds that could support human will. That was the original intent of the Life Carrier's formula.

"About one million years ago, evolution and the Life Carrier patterns finally produced their intended fruit: the first humans. They emerged, as intended, from the higher primates. The original humans, a pair of twins, male and female, were capable of something their purely animal relatives lacked. They were able to use wisdom and foresight as no animal can. And they were inclined to worship, a new impulse that was also a part of the Life Carriers' plan to lift and enlighten humanity.

"A half-billion years of evolution, including some mysterious and 'sudden' mutations along the way, produced a very special brother and sister. As the twins grew, they increasingly rejected their less intelligent parents and family; they finally ran away. These two, Andon and Fonta, were the first creatures on Earth to possess a capacity for spirit recognition, and an awareness of self-consciousness of being. Their exceptional minds were the first to employ *wisdom* and, among other advances such as primitive language, used it in the creation and maintenance of fire. And they were the first humans to *worship* the creator of fire and Earth. Wisdom and worship set humans apart from the animals.

"Upon their birth the Earth was placed on the universe records as producing personal beings capable of conscious awareness and freewill—humans who could worship and who possessed wisdom. Andon and Fonta are a true mother and father to all human beings.

"Half a million years after evolution had produced the first humans, ones who were physically, mentally, and spiritually ready, the Earth was ripe for elementary revealed truth. That is when the Planetary Prince arrived, bringing myself, and ninety-nine other volunteer ascenders. We all took origin on different worlds within our system."

Another time, Van told his students, "When a world has progressed, after human consciousness and the power to know and choose God appears, the first in a series of divine visitations occurs. An administrator and his staff are sent to enlighten and rule humanity until Adam and Eve come with their unique contribution of biological uplift.

"After the Earth received the Prince and his entourage, progress was slow but sure for nearly 300,000 years. Gradual and important advances were being made. But then, with little warning, a rebellion broke out in the local system's ranks. A high administrator, Lucifer by name, denied the existence of God the Father and led many of his subordinates to believe this lie. As a consequence, the administrative staff of thirty-seven inhabited worlds, including Earth and many of its attending angels, went astray.

"Earth's Prince went over to the rebel cause and our administration fractured into loyalists and rebels. But Amadon and I, and some of our colleagues did not join the rebellion. As soon as it broke out the disloyal ones began making mischief. They roved the planet creating endless trouble and causing serious confusion.

"After seven years with no resolution, nor any admission of error, Amadon and I abandoned the rebels and the world's fallen Prince. While they were creating chaos and discord, we carved out the core of the Tree of Life and made our way to the highlands of Asia.

"We remained in those far mountains until the planetary inspectors arrived and settled on the three possible sites for the new Garden. Before their visit, Amadon and I were kept informed by loyal angels about the 'war in heaven.' It went on for seven years. But the consequences are still working themselves out a hundred and sixty thousand years later, on the Earth and the other thirty-six fallen worlds. During that time Amadon and I waited for humanity to reach its physical peak so that an Adam and Eve could be dispatched and begin repairing the damage done by the Prince's betrayal.

"The violet race brings not only increased physical vigor and spiritual capacity to their assigned world, it also fosters the appreciation and creation of music, humor, and artistic expression. And with this vastly increased creativity, with this greater physical and intellectual power, there begins a great age of scientific and technological achievement, followed by even greater ages of spiritual advancement."

As the day's festivities reached their inevitable end, as the glorious red, purple, and orange sunset waned, Van beseeched those still lingering to depart for the night, so as to give the newly arrived pair "time to acclimate, to adapt, to breathe in the Garden's fine aromas."

Adam and Eve were very gracious in bidding their admirers a fond goodnight. Eve said to all in her charming manner, "Go to your rest faithful friends, for there is much to do tomorrow, and many tomorrows thereafter, during which we shall come to know each other as one great and affectionate family."

Adam added, "We thank one and all for preparing this beautiful Garden and for this loving reception. Your good labors will never be forgotten, and they shall ever be counted as righteousness. Rest you well!" With that, most of the group dispersed and went to their shelters.

The dozen or so who remained refused to be dismissed. They sought simply to be near Adam and Eve. Van was about to ask them to depart when Eve stepped forward, approaching a little boy holding his father's hand. He looked up at her, wide-eyed and smiling. She came down on one knee, then slowly and gently took the boy into her arms and stood. Somehow everyone there felt as if they had been embraced and lifted.

"Back in our heavenly home, Adam and I have many children and grandchildren, not unlike this little one," Eve said to the father. The boy looked as if he had been hugged by God! The father smiled but was too awed to speak. After that tender moment, Eve set the boy down, saying, "May the silent stars and this beautiful sky attend your dreams. We bid you all good night and good rest."

All then began drifting their way home thinking only of tomorrow when they might be near this magical pair again. But only the children slept after that dramatic day. The adults who had met and talked with Adam or Eve marveled at their good fortune, up until the sun rose. All night they discussed the phenomenal events of that unforgettable day, pledging to remember its details and promising to tell their children.

And what a day it had been! The Garden volunteers and guests had witnessed an epochal occurrence. Many of them, at some point, had an opportunity to come near, even greet and be touched by these two god-like beings.

It wasn't long before everyone realized Eve and Adam were especially fond of, and attuned to, the physical and intellectual needs of children. People were genuinely touched by the graciousness and warmth shown to all children by Eve and Adam. And everyone was moved by the couple's unmistakable and kindly demeanor so lovingly and repeatedly extended to people of every age.

Chapter 4

FIRST NIGHT

As they strolled the Garden under the glistening light of the rising moon, the pair conversed briefly with Van and Amadon, then Lyla and Lam.

Adam said to Van and Amadon, "Your faithfulness and service are known throughout all Nebadon. Van, it is well noted on high that you and Amadon have remained loyal for 1600 lonely centuries on this sphere, toiling without complaint, even under the isolation of quarantine. You will receive well-deserved acclaim when you leave here. Eve and I thank you for such selfless, unflagging loyalty and persistent labors before our coming.

"The Garden appears to be in the best possible condition considering the difficulties and delays you must surely have encountered on a world still in rebellion. We are hoping you might remain a while to overlap our administrations. Ere long however, you will be released to go where we were a short time ago, where everyone knows of your good works and staunch devotion on this isolated and backward planet. You are well known across Nebadon as 'Van the Steadfast.'"

Eve said to Amadon, "Good and true Amadon, you should know there is a question that personalities across the universe ask when this world is discussed: 'What of Amadon? Does he remain unmoved?' Be prepared for great honors when you arrive on Jerusem, both of you, for you have proven yourselves worthy of them."

The four exchanged warm embraces. Van and Amadon departed, their spirits lifted by the success of the day. Lam and

Lyla stood by in silent witness, their hearts and minds filled with affectionate wonder as never before. Adam said to them, "Perhaps your first assignment should be to lead us to our home."

Lyla replied, "Of course!" and added, "Van told us you would want to rest close by the Father's Temple on this first night. Our preparation team built a cottage for your comfort, in addition to your estate in the east of Eden."

Lam then humbly asked, "We were wondering, by what names should we call you?"

Eve answered, "We wish to convey a sense of familiarity and availability to everyone. Therefore, we don't approve of titles. We were given personal names at our birth long ago, but they would be meaningless here and difficult to pronounce."

Adam added, "You may call us by our sonship designation for the time being: Adam and Eve; we require and request no titles." The first Lyla and Lam reported being completely dazzled and charmed in the couple's presence, by their obvious modesty and understated humility.

As they walked, Adam asked, "Were you both born in the Garden?"

Lam replied, "We were. Lyla's family and mine came to the Garden after Van's committee visited our village to seek volunteers, almost a hundred years ago. Our families have lived here since then. Van said we are, 'the goodness of the Earth,' and he chose many like us to settle here."

Before anything else was said, Lyla asked, from wonder and curiosity, "How long have you been alive? Van wasn't sure."

Eve and Adam laughed. What a beautiful sound it made. Lam and Lyla never forgot it. Eve answered, "Too many years to say. We just completed a 15,000 Earth-year assignment in the system's life laboratories."

Adam asked, "Did Van tell you about where we lived and worked before coming to the Earth?" Before they could reply, he inquired further, "Now tell us, what all has Van revealed to you and your fellows?"

Lyla answered first, "Grandmother said Van first taught that there is one God who created everything and made a plan including everyone. He told her our God is like a great father who loves all his children everywhere. To make his plan work God sends his more advanced children to guide the evolving worlds like ours to a time of 'Light and Life.' But something happened to the Earth. Van said wisdom was forgotten, and the ones sent to help humans caused us great harm. Those erring leaders rebelled against God and ruined the divine plans. Van teaches everyone that you were being sent to correct the problems of the rebellion and reestablish God's rightful rule that was stolen away by the selfish rebels."

Lam continued, "Van said you lived on Jerusem, in beautiful homes made to raise children, and with great gardens to grow food and flowers. He said we would visit the homes of the Adams and Eves after we die and go to the mansion worlds, the first heaven… And he said that the mansions are all round, like a coconut. He taught us the Earth is round too.

"He told us the mansion worlds spin around a bigger world, and that world goes around one even bigger. He said these special worlds are constructed, like we are building Eden, and they have days and nights, even years, but no sun. There is no bad weather, and no home needs a roof."

Lyla added, "He teaches in the Garden's schools that Adams and Eves are born, grow to be adults, then raise their little ones on that biggest world. Van said that he has been to all the mansion worlds, and many others. He said there are worlds like Earth throughout the universe. He told us those worlds are perfect compared to the Earth, that no creature must eat another to live; and there is no fear. My family's children beg Van to tell stories about the mansion worlds. He knows many stories, he is very old."

Lyla then asked, "How can Lam and I be sure we will go to the mansions when we die? Van teaches us to believe and trust, that everyone who believes without seeing will go. We are learning to have faith in things we can't see, that God can be trusted even if we don't see him. But that has become a lot easier now that we have seen you! You've been alive so long, you must have seen God. What does he look like?"

Adam responded, "No Lyla, Eve and I have not seen God in person, nor have we been in God's personal presence. But we have met former mortals, just like you, who have been to Paradise, received the embrace of the Universal Father, and returned to the universes of time and space to serve their ascending brethren; they offer proof that it is possible to meet God at the center of all creation. If you are not certain that God exists, you will be after meeting them."

Eve said softly, "And we know God exists because all else exists. Our Father requires us to believe, to love, and to trust. So, God must be loved to be known. Can a loving being reveal him or herself to a loveless one?"

Adam told them, "There are many inhabited spheres in the Father's universe. You can see right here in Eden how beautiful even a troubled one can be. I must say, you and your workmates created this in a remarkably brief period. If such beauty can exist here with less than a century's work, imagine what the Earth might be in a thousand centuries. Now take your imagination even higher and visualize the beauty and grandeur that comes about on worlds that have been visited by several orders of the sons and daughters of God over vast stretches of time. Then think of how you are designed and destined to fill a unique role in this eternal unfolding. Do not doubt it."

Eve then asked, "What else has Van told you and the Garden workers about the administrator who came before us, the Planetary Prince who joined the rebellion?"

Lam answered, "Van and Amadon warn everyone all the time that the rebels are invisible but they're still here and still causing trouble. He said they already lost their authority and don't have any power over us unless we choose to give it. He told us that someday the rebels will be taken away for a merciful reckoning. And he said God would forgive them if they asked, but he thinks some of them never will."

"And that may be true," Adam lamented. "Rebellion, then war, broke out at the system level. Many of the lower level celestial personalities also went to the rebel's cause, even before the Earth's administrators strayed."

Eve said, "It appears that Van has prepared you to resist any temptation for their cause. We are very thankful to have you as our personal aides. You have attended Van's schools, acquired the ability to reason, and to read and write. We are fortunate that you are able to create and keep oral and written records of the events of the Garden for humanity's sake. Do not hesitate to ask us about the details of what transpires here. We want the record to be as accurate as possible."

After a moment Lyla told the pair, "Van has already created an outdoor theater, a ways from the Father's Temple. He wants us to train some of our family to tell your story to the Garden's children. And to groups of visitors from all the lands outside. There will be many more visitors now that you're here. Amadon created a team of workers who provide tools for writing, so we may always keep records to consult and to build on. Van wants everyone to read and write."

Lam said, "We intend to have our children make copies. These will be given to the temple leaders and schoolmasters. Van suggested this, so they can consult the records anytime. He wants the schools and the priests to teach the same ideals, as well as Earth's history. The original we should always keep in a safe place, with trusted family members. We are honored to have this role. People of the future will want to know about the things you do, and what living on the Earth can be like when there are good, wise leaders."

Adam said, "Let your record reflect the true and unending story, begun here in the Garden, recorded by you and your children. In this way, always will there be an accurate account by which to measure, validate, or eliminate, all other accounts. Having both oral and written accounts, with copies freely available to all, should ensure the records' safekeeping and accuracy.

"Eve and I know many stories—some true and some not—will result from our arrival and mission. Because your family will live close to ours you will have intimate knowledge of all that we do. We think it would be good if you create a large family to insure a continuous line of aides and recorders. We want to keep you, and your descendants, informed of all our decisions and acts so that a truthful record of life in the Garden is kept on Earth for all time. Therefore, you should feel free to ask us about anything."

"We want a big family," Lyla declared, Lam quickly agreeing.

Eve smiled and said, "Then we have a common goal."

For a moment all four reflected on the nature and value of this first private conversation. Lam and Lyla were already feeling at ease, and very pleased to find Eve and Adam so approachable, knowledgeable, and unpretentious.

When they arrived at the temporary lodging Lam and Lyla bid them good night and went to rest in a small room adjacent to the kitchen. But they were too energized to sleep, and overhearing Adam and Eve was more important than rest. Neither pair realized Amadon and his men were secretly guarding the cottage.

Eve and Adam sat at a central stone table discussing details of their situation, planning and steadying their resolve. Lam and Lyla heard most of what Eve and Adam said before the pair finally retired to their bedchamber.

It was here, in the quiet of the night, that the pair first felt the remoteness and loneliness of a quarantined world. Owing to the rebellion, there was no means of direct interplanetary communication. Here they were separated from their family and former friends, cut-off from all that was familiar, set down on a confused, disordered world, and expected to lead the primitive races up from untold millennia of darkness. The weight of this gigantic challenge was now upon them and their offspring.

When sleep wouldn't come to their new bodies, Eve and Adam decided to go for a walk in the moonlit Garden. Amid this shimmering Earthly beauty of the night season, a soft warm breeze caressed them. It had been a joyful and celebratory day, but thoughts of the many difficulties and harsh trials of future days swirled in their minds. They walked and talked well into the night, as loneliness hung in the air.

After overhearing Adam and Eve's discussion, and then seeing them walking alone, Lam and Lyla became concerned. They had not previously realized the diverse difficulties, scope, and complexity of the Adamic mission. In the absence of sleep, they prayed to be up to their task of supporting and assisting their new rulers. At the same time, out in the Garden, Eve and Adam prayed for wisdom and fortitude, and then fell into worshipful communion until the dawn light appeared.

Chapter 5

SECOND DAY

This day brought another full schedule. Van had arranged a meeting between the Melchizedek receivers and Adam and Eve. He and Amadon called on them early. The pair knew a meeting with the twelve receivers would be one of their first orders of business and were expecting this would be the day.

Before the Adamic pair came, Van taught both teachers and students that: "The first will creatures evolved a million years ago. They took origin in the Life Carriers' implants over a half-billion years before that.

"After the Life Carriers do their work, evolution begins its work. Life goes through many changes before human will appears. When it does, the planetary observers call for the first order of sonship, the Planetary Prince. The Princes are always the first in a series of divinely appointed administrators.

"The mission of the Prince and his staff is scientific, intellectual, and spiritual. Each visitation of a divine son or daughter takes the will-creatures and the planet's culture one step higher. The highest step is perfection, personal and planetary perfection.

"Achieving perfection requires wisdom, and wisdom is derived from experience, successes and failures. This is true for both descending and ascending children of God, especially those living and serving on rebellion tinged worlds."

Before they left, Eve said to Lyla and Lam, "Come with us. We want you to observe this meeting. Afterward we will make a permanent, detailed record. Do not concern yourselves about today's meal, Amadon's helpers will arrange everything." He was also present at this meeting, which was being held in a large private chamber of the Father's Temple.

The Melchizedek council was fully represented; all twelve receivers were present. And though Lyla and Lam saw no physical forms and heard no words from the Melchizedeks, they could sense a majestic presence when Adam, Eve, Van, or Amadon were engaged in conversation with them.

After the meeting Eve recalled, and had Lyla record, the Melchizedek spokesmen's opening statement: "The council welcomes the Adamic son and daughter to Earth. We are pleased finally to witness the inauguration of the next order of sonship on this fallen world. As you know, the Father's rule has been rejected on this quarantined sphere. It must be reinstated, and the light of truth restored. Take heed our advice and admonitions, for you will be tested, and severely so."

Eve told Lyla the first business of this meeting was to offer her and Adam intimate details of the planet's history and the rebels still roaming it. They listened and discussed at length the past, present, and future consequences of the iniquity of the previous world leaders. Eve said the rebellion was very much alive and still playing out, on the Earth, and on the other fallen worlds.

During the latter part of the day the group went over the Garden's master plan as had been painstakingly drafted by Van and Amadon. Adam and Eve were warned repeatedly that mischievous ones were still practicing their evil, and that they should not be trusted in any way, measure, or form. They were invisible to mortal inhabitants, but with their extended vision, Adam, Eve, Van, and Amadon could view the rebel leaders and their subordinates, even if humans could not. Many rebels dared to be present at this meeting, lurking ominously in the background. They were well known to Van, Amadon, and the receivers.

"You may as well meet them now," Van said to Adam and Eve. Turning to the lurkers, he commanded, "Come forward you cowards! Greet the world's new leaders. You know what this means. You have been deposed."

Nothing happened.

Van goaded them, "Your reign of rebellion is over! A Son and Daughter have been sent by the Most Highs, coming from where I once was, where Amadon and I shall soon go. But you! There is a prison world awaiting you... It is well that you fear this august council."

After a long moment, there was no reply. The dark rebels shied away from the brilliance of the venerable personalities at the meeting. They especially feared and avoided the Melchizedeks.

Van went back to admonishing Eve and Adam, saying emphatically, "They will come around again when the Melchizedeks and I have gone. They will pretend to be your devoted friends and willing helpers. Ignore their poison words and tainted charms, for they love not the Truth. They may no longer believe it exists."

The chief Melchizedek pointed again to the invisibility problem, saying to Adam and Eve, "Never cease warning your subjects about these rebels whom they cannot see. Your tasks will be made all the more difficult and vexing by these nefarious pretenders. Your wisdom, patience, even your faith will be tested, tried, and pushed to their limits, perhaps beyond. You must fortify yourselves with patience and wisdom.

"We trust you will not fail," Melchizedek told the pair. "Listen always to the 'Voice in the Garden,' your abiding angel, Solonia. And never forget these angels are loaned to Adams and Eves to assure that you will remain true to the mission— ever keeping you within the safe bounds set for such grand and difficult endeavors as planetary transformation. All the more difficult on a world tinged by rebellion.

"Solonia and her helpers, in combination with the midwayers, will assist you. Both groups are working behind the scenes in the lives of the men and women of Earth, fostering brotherhood and the establishment of good families at every social and administrative level, thereby countering the work of the rebels. Do not succumb to doubts about whether the master plan will work. It will, given enough time. Patience must always be your ally in this endeavor.

"You know the Earth's history, littered with awful woe, bitter chaos, and the destructive confusion that took hold in the aftermath of the rebellion. Almost all the social and spiritual advances achieved by the Prince's administration during the 300,000 years of his reign were lost. We receivers were informed that, before coming to the Earth, you were admonished about the problems and troubles to be encountered on this rebellion tainted world. Those warnings cannot be overstated."

The events of the 162,000 years since the rebellion's outbreak were much discussed and closely examined for valuable lessons. All throughout Adam and Eve were reminded to be on guard, not to give in to the same unbridled liberty and wicked sophistry to which the rebels and their subordinates had succumbed.

The Melchizedek chief admonished them one final time, "Ever be aware and do not fall into forgetfulness when faced with seemingly endless defeat and repeated discouragement.

Sooner or later, the rebels will be tried and removed. Their misguided mission has already failed. Someday, if you do not falter, this Garden will grow to be the most beautiful center of spiritual civilization this world has ever seen. Never permit your mission to mix with the lies and confusion that have so disrupted progress here. Already have Van and Amadon made a good start on the path to rehabilitation. But you cannot let down your guard. You may be certain trouble awaits. Vigilance must be your watchword.

"Hear me when I advise you to permit the infusion of the Adamic heritage to do most of the work of accelerating planetary progress. Over the next several thousand years concentrate your focus on building up your family and improving the Garden. Maintain stability with a steady hand across the centuries and make changes gradually.

"Do not fall victim to *any* preemptive social engineering of your own design that would attempt to shorten time or override necessary processes. That was the error of your predecessors, the willful disregard of the preordained plan of progress."

All Melchizedeks signaled agreement when their chief reiterated the tried and true lesson of the ages that, short-sighted good intentions do not always bring about righteous or lasting solutions. And the pair was once more reminded not to attempt biologic uplift—not to allow Adamic interbreeding with the planet's natives, until their family was at least one half million in number. "And let there be no exceptions," said Melchizedek, "a default will be declared if in any manner you ignore or disobey this rule."

Lastly, Van gave Adam and Eve a status account of the Garden saying, "The Edenic peninsula was designed to accommodate one million inhabitants. There is, as you have surely realized, much work yet to be done. Amadon, the Garden laborers, and I, have only five percent of the Garden under full cultivation. Another fifteen to twenty percent is partially cultivated. At present, there are twelve thousand miles of roads and paths. We built thousands of stone and brick buildings. Our plan specified that there be no more than seven houses in a cluster. And there are thousands of miles of irrigation canals and ditches to supplement the dews that nourish the Garden each morn.

"The water and sanitation systems are in place. After severe water-borne illnesses occurred, I finally convinced everyone of the need to protect the drinking water system. For now, all waste matter is buried. Amadon has a team of inspectors who make daily rounds to ensure the purity of the drinking water and the proper burial of waste and disease agents. Plans are to create a disposal system that carries away the Garden's waste, with your approval, of course.

"We have gathered the most intelligent and far-seeing of the surrounding tribes to serve as your administrators and field workers. Some families have lived here for four generations. We also gathered, crossbred, and thereby improved some grains, fruits, and nuts from this region. We now leave all this in your hands, including the furnishing of your residence in the east. We thought it only proper to leave your home unadorned, that this be reserved for your choices, and in your good time.

"You know the Garden sits on a peninsula. Perhaps you have also been informed there is a defensive wall across the peninsula's neck. And there is a lesser wall beyond it. In between the two is a twelve-section animal preserve—habitats for plants and beasts of the region. This double wall arrangement has twelve gates connected to twelve sheltered paths that run between the walls. The gates are well guarded and are the only way into the Garden. The encircling mountains should prevent any attempt to invade the peninsula."

Adam said, "Van, your thorough preparations provide an excellent beginning. We learned some of what you presented today, on Jerusem. And from what we have so far observed on the Earth, we are entirely pleased with your work. You and Amadon have done very well. Already is the Garden landscaped and producing. It is also secure. Eve and I will study the Garden's master plan more. We intend to make only modest changes, for the present time at least."

Eve told Van, "Because of your extensive and thoughtful preparations, your long labors and tireless determination, our work has been made easier. For now, we can offer only our gratitude as a token of our pledge to carry on in this same vein, to follow through with what you have so well begun."

Van added, "We also have taken the first steps in the execution of the long-term plan to spread Garden culture to the lands beyond. With the help of many loyalists, we have been able to establish more than a hundred Edenic outposts in nearby settlements."

Then he said to the pair, with great concern in his voice, "What Amadon, others, and I have done is but a modest beginning. I can report there is a developing cohesion among those hundred outposts already established. But that aspect of the plan needs continual attention.

"You will find the concepts and practices of representative governance far too advanced for most of the tribes and villages. For now, simply tell them what you want. They respect authority just as long as you maintain their trust and inspire their confidence. More than that, engender trade and more trade. Already we have begun manufacturing, and various schools of trade. We barter with metal-works, pottery, and foodstuffs. And we freely teach these skills to outsiders wanting to learn. Their fellows are deeply impressed when Garden visitors return with newly acquired skills and laborsaving devices. Especially do they appreciate and wish to learn our methods of producing superior pottery and a variety of metalworks."

Thus ended the formal discussions after which attendees conferred informally. The presence of the Melchizedeks was a welcome reminder of Adam and Eve's former life on Jerusem, with its diverse population of beings of many orders.

The meeting raised the pair's spirits, and their resolve. But they also hoped the Melchizedeks would remain on Earth many years to guide and advise them. On leaving the temple Van walked with Adam and Eve. He brought out more details and possible remedies for the multifaceted difficulties that had so recently been transferred onto Adam and Eve's shoulders. Lyla and Lam followed behind, hearing and planning to record this conversation. Eve was always more than willing to assist them in their record-making task. Her memory was excellent. She recounted, word for word, the advice from the Melchizedeks, and the facts Van offered.

Van wished very much to share all his acquired knowledge of the planet's peoples and their various levels of understanding. But it would require more time. He said, in part, "We took great pains to select the best men and women from the neighboring tribes to help you administer the expansion of the Garden. Most of them are of Nodite lineage. We brought potential leaders and their children here for training and education eight decades ago, but still their grasp of divine realities is elementary. Their understanding is confused by ignorance and pre-conceived notions.

"Once more, let me say they respond best to a firm hand. When they are convinced of your right to authority, they will, in general, prove loyal, diligent, and hard working. But we discovered long ago, the vast majority of the people on this planet have little inclination to self-govern. To a fault they will look to you for authoritarian leadership and superhuman wisdom. Take care not to overawe them. Having witnessed your welcoming ceremony yesterday, they are now prone to fall down before you, to see you as gods come to Earth.

"I repeat yet again, ask not what your subjects want, rather tell them and their appointed leaders what you desire. Show them how, and then command them to perform it. You will find this method best for the time being. Democratic, representative governance is a strange idea to most. It must be introduced later, gradually, and after much education."

Van sought to reassure them, "Fret not, dear brother and sister, Amadon, the Melchizedek council, and I will remain on the Earth—for several years, if needed." Eve and Adam felt immense relief and took great comfort in hearing those words.

They returned to thank the Melchizedeks, then left the temple. Van said, "Tomorrow we thought a grand tour of your new domains is in order. Without objection, in the morning, we fly!" Adam and Eve knew that meant the fandors were trained and ready to take them for an aerial view of the Garden.

Adam replied, "We both very much enjoyed riding the passenger birds over the Adamic estates back on Jerusem." He and Eve were delighted to hear they would soon fly the skies of the Earth on the backs of the great winged creatures.

When they arrived at their temporary dwelling that evening, Van and Amadon wished the pair good rest and hopeful dreams. Van went to the Father's Temple, but Amadon did not follow. Instead he and his lieutenants set up a watch around Adam and Eve's cottage, ordering his men, "Take care you are not seen, we do not wish to alarm those we guard."

When they had settled, Lyla asked Eve about her experience with the "war in heaven" before coming to Earth. Van had, long ago, revealed this war to his students who were asking about the system's history, and how he came to be stranded so long on Earth.

Lyla learned that Adam and Eve believed self-glorification, personal pride, and administrative impatience were the cause of the rebellion. Eve told her, "Because of our training, because of the trust we have in our superiors, and because of our faith in the goodness and watch-care of God, the rebellion was never a threat to Adam or me. But we understood the need to be wary of the deceits of the rebellious leaders and their followers. It was obvious, to some of us at least, that the rebels were abusing their personal and public trust. It was a blatant betrayal of trust and a denial of Our Father's sovereignty."

Chapter 6

FIRST MEAL

On entering their temporary residence, Adam and Eve found several baskets of ripe fruit and bowls of shelled nuts spread out on a long broad stone table. The food had been produced within the Garden's grounds and offered according to prior instructions from Lyla, who had been tutored by Van on the dietary preferences of the pair. Eve and Adam had only tasted certain foods since taking up life in their new bodies. This would be their first full meal.

"Excellent!" Adam called out as he and Eve eyed the buffet. "Come, join us."

Lyla and Lam were deeply honored that they alone would share this first meal with these godlike beings fresh from heaven.

The pair began by sampling each fruit and nut. And while they declared them nutritious and tasty, they discussed ways to improve flavor, nutrition, size, color, seed content, and rate of production. Lam and Lyla listened in fascination as the pair discussed possibilities and potentials for crossbreeding and grafting.

After a while Lyla asked, "How do you know all this about our foods? And do you wish to have only one meal a day? What time of day do you prefer to take your meals? May we eat foods other than you eat?"

Eve answered, "Lyla, our training, for many thousands of years, was in experimental biology. On Jerusem we learned about the plant and animal life that exists on the inhabited worlds of the system.

"We will eat once daily, near midday. You already know that only fruits and nuts from the Garden shall be our diet. I will gather the leaves and fruit from the Tree of Life. Your family may eat that which your bodies require; the early generations of our family will consume only foods grown in the Garden."

Lam said, "In the Garden's school, Van taught everybody about the system headquarters, Jerusem. He said it's the central world for six hundred worlds like Earth. And he always told us that we will be citizens there someday, after we die and resurrect in a new body, one that doesn't ever die."

Adam replied to Lam saying, "And there you will learn, just as we did, about the awe-inspiring diversity, the intricate web of plant and animal life found on all evolutionary worlds. These higher spheres, like Jerusem and Edentia, are intended to be models for such worlds—just as we are all derived from models and patterns inherent in the infinite creativity of our divine parents. You will be astounded by the wonders of your future adventure, my friends. Now tell us about your families. Do your parents and grandparents still live and do they abide in the Garden?"

Eve asked, "And do you have siblings?"

Lyla answered, "You know Lam and I were raised inside the Garden. Our children will be the fifth generation born here. Our two families have always been close. All our grandparents who were born in the Garden are still alive. I have five brothers and four sisters. Lam has four of each. We grew up knowing each other, playing and working together. But we took special notice of each other when we came of age."

Eve brightened at the thought and asked, "But you are not yet married?"

"We want to," Lam answered.

Lyla said, "But we waited. We hoped you and Adam would marry us. Van said you do such things."

"It will be our honor," said Eve. "It is customary that Eves and Adams officiate at weddings. Tomorrow we will send out a call for all garden couples who wish to marry. Adam and I have discussed this already; we plan to make marriages a regular event of Garden life. Let's begin with once a month... The more there are, the more our joy. It will be an occasion for Garden celebrations, music and dancing, playing and performing. And it is perfectly appropriate that our personal aides be in the first group to wed."

Lyla and Lam leapt together in a joyful embrace and both then bowed to the pair in over-flowing gratitude for such thrilling news. "Oh, thank you. It will be the best day of our lives," said Lyla. Lam beamed in agreement.

Adam then asked, "How often have you been outside the Garden gates? Van informed us that you are worthy ambassadors."

Lam replied, "He takes us outside when he needs help making friends and finding traders. Before we grew up, we went with our parents and grandparents. We've helped find lots of friends, and traders. We even found some good leaders to bring into the Garden. Lyla and I learned about keeping peace with the tribes on the mainland. He teaches everyone that trading is important for peace. And for your plans to make all the Earth a garden of peace."

"The Garden must be like heaven." Lyla declared. "Van said the whole world could be as good except for people disagreeing and fighting over who's right. There are a few workers here, they make trouble on purpose. Some are just that way, but some are secretly working against us. The midwayers know everything about them; they tell Van what they see and hear. He lets most of the trouble-makers stay because they could be causing even more problems out there. He said some will join our side after working in the Garden and seeing how good and right it is here. Most of us live in harmony, by what Van taught us about God and prayer and worship. Everyone is amazed how his teachings changed some of the biggest warriors into leaders, inside and outside the Garden. We do have spies and enemies working in the Garden, but there are many more wise and loyal leaders. Not like outside Eden."

Adam then said, "Van and Amadon have indeed set a high standard for wise, effective leadership. We know the midwayers will keep us informed about mischief-makers within and without, ones we will convert in time. Eve and I believe Van's plan is good and his methods worthy. We won't change them unless different and better ways are found."

Eve, the very embodiment of motherhood, added, "The Garden needs more children. Very soon we will have little ones, ours and yours." She lifted her hands in prayer, saying, "May our two families live long and be fruitful. Adam and I intend to begin creating our new family very soon."

Lyla asked, "Van said that you had children where you were before. Very many?"

Adam answered, "We were parents to exactly one hundred. They were the last ones to bid us farewell before our journey to the Earth. They may still be celebrating our planetary assignment."

Then, with motherly emotion, Eve lamented, "I miss them so..."

"Are there fifty boys and fifty girls?" Lyla asked.

"Yes, Lyla," Eve replied. "But all have grown-up and are involved in projects and activities somewhere in the system. Every one of them has taken a position of trust and responsibility." She shed a tear through a smile. Adam moved to her side.

After a moment of reflection Eve and Adam returned to the meal. As they tasted one item after another, they talked of their long lives on Jerusem. Adam spoke with fondness about their personal estate where some of their children still reside. Eve said this is where she and Adam will someday return, but as glorified beings who have successfully transformed a world beset by rank savagery and blinding ignorance into a sphere of sublime creativity and God-knowing.

Lyla and Lam were astonished by how much the pair ate. It was after all, their first meal and they were empty. Their aides might have stayed up all night asking Adam and Eve questions and hearing their replies, but after a while Lyla sensed it was time to leave their masters and rest.

Lyla told Eve, "We would leave you for the night, but please call on us for any reason, any at all." She and Eve embraced warmly as Adam and Lam looked on, adoring their mates. Both pairs were feeling good about this new association of two humans working for and with two visitors sent by God. At the end of this extraordinary day, Eve and Adam felt certain Van had chosen the right ones to be their aides.

But the pair couldn't stop feeling the loneliness of having no children at hand, neither sight nor sound of a grandchild. That night they sorely missed the familiarity and conveniences of their grand estate back on Jerusem, a sphere whereon trillions of beings of every imaginable kind and type interacted with them and their children, by day and by night.

Adam nor Eve felt like sleeping. They decided on another moonlit walk, to discuss the serious challenges of their situation, so vividly presented during the meeting earlier that day. They needed to hear each other's ideas now that they were face to face with the hard facts of isolation and the manifold difficulties of rebellion. Most of that second night they reviewed their problems and considered workable solutions. It was just before daybreak when they finally returned to the cottage, on the morning of the third day.

As they entered, Adam hugged Eve and asked, "When shall we move to our permanent residence, a real home wherein to raise our first son, and a mere half-million thereafter?" She smiled affectionately and in a soft voice responded, "And how is it you know our first born will be a male?" The pair retired to their bed-chamber.

Chapter 7

THIRD DAY

It was mid-morning when Van and Amadon appeared at the cottage's door. Eve and Adam were up and preparing to tour the Garden—not on the ground but in the air.

There once lived giant, intelligent birds, large enough to carry a full-grown passenger. These clever creatures had been trained and stabled on a low hilltop not far from the Father's Temple. They were strong and could be ridden all day if required. They could also fly at night, if the moon was giving light.

"It's not far to the birds' roost," Amadon told them.

"We are almost ready," Eve replied. "Come in! Lyla made a tea."

Lyla strained aromatic leaves that had been soaking overnight in a clay vessel. She filled six wooden cups and Lam carried them to the table.

Eve and Adam came out and greeted everyone. After they sat at tea, Van asked in jest, "Will you recall how to fly a bird properly?"

Eve replied in kind, "Do not doubt it, 'Van the Steadfast.'" He laughed.

Adam smiled saying, "I am very much looking forward to the flight. Are you able to accompany us, Amadon?"

"I had planned to."

On the way to the aviary, Lyla and Lam listened in fascination as the others discussed various features of the

Garden. Eve commented on its appearance and condition, "You and the Garden residents have done such marvelous work, landscaping and beautification. It is a precious advantage that irrigation is well in hand. But the morning mists do most of the work watering, do they not? And I have seen no evidence of dangerous beasts on the loose."

Adam then asked, "Is there such a heavy dew every morn, all year?"

Amadon replied, "Almost every morning. The dews and the irrigation channels make rain all but unnecessary. You will clearly see from above, the network of canals the workers dug. And what is left to do."

As they ambled along the path up to the bird's roost Eve called out many of the plants and their identifiers. She spoke of their properties, of their nutritional and medicinal uses. Lyla and Lam bagged the seed samples she collected.

On arriving at the launch and laying eyes on the fandors, Adam said in amazement, "Such exquisite creatures!"

Eve approached one slowly, with outstretched hand. The giant birds were immediately fascinated by her and not in the least shy. "These creatures are quite clever, aren't they?" The birds appeared to understand her as two moved in close, nuzzling her gently with their enormous beaks. "And affectionate too."

"These creatures are known for their remarkable abilities," Eve said as she touched them. "They are extremely powerful and only want to please. They can travel great distances carrying one, even two, passengers. They are well known for being intelligent, servile, and very friendly. They have wide-ranging vocal ability. They can remember and speak scores of words."

To everyone's surprise, one of the pair nuzzling Eve spoke out saying only one word, "You." The other creature looked intensely into Eve's eyes asking. "You like?"

"Yes, I like you," replied Eve, stroking their massive necks with each hand.

This instant and fearless bonding amazed the lead handler; it was beyond anything he had ever seen. He took a step forward and said in utter humility and deference, "You have touched their minds and hearts, Lady."

She smiled saying, "They are in excellent condition. I sense they are happy here. You and your helpmates are to be congratulated."

"Thank you, Lady. Everyone working at the stable is very thankful to serve the Garden in this way. May I know how many to equip?"

"Six, including Lyla and Lam," Adam said. The trainer seemed confused and took Lyla aside asking, "When the birds are prepared, should I offer to instruct Eve and Adam?"

Everyone overheard the question and laughed in good nature. Van answered, "You are a thoughtful caretaker, but do not be concerned. They both have much experience and training, on even greater birds than these. Concern yourself not, good and faithful keeper."

The keeper then led the birds to the launch area where they were readied. After the six had mounted the beasts, he and his helpers closely and carefully inspected the saddles and reins of each bird. Then the head trainer looked up at the sky and out over the plains, noting wind direction. He pointed and gave a command. Without hesitation all six flyers moved into position, facing the wind and spreading their gigantic wings.

Another command was given. All birds launched themselves at once, flattening and stiffening their wings, diving sharply and flying close to the hillside to pick up speed. When they sensed proper velocity had been reached, the birds fully extended those huge feathered wings, flapping hard and rising quickly. They expended tremendous effort and all six were soon well above the launch point, gliding effortlessly by comparison.

As they soared, Adam and Eve peered down on the long, wide Garden valley with the lush green mountains rising all around. The Father's Temple and its large courtyard were the most prominent features.

The passengers could plainly see the Garden's expanse occupying an oval basin sitting in the center of a massive peninsula that extended westward from the eastern shores of the Mediterranean Basin. They observed four main rivers gathering waters from the many tributaries pouring off the encircling mountains. Those rivers joined to form one great river that flowed east across the valley's broad plain, passing through the peninsular neck flowing into the Euphrates valley and on out to sea.

Amadon called out, as he pointed, "You can see how much roadwork and irrigation is complete."

The midwayers once told Van this peninsula was the most beautiful of all natural settings on Earth. With the improvements made in preparation for Adam and Eve, it had the potential to become an Earthly paradise, a fitting place to build an advanced civilization from which to send out their children to enlighten the world.

Lyla recorded Adam and Eve's spirits soaring during this flight, as they more fully realized the actual work that had been done, and the tremendous potential of their vast and beautiful new home. Virtually an island it was, a secure and safe sanctuary for raising little ones and beginning their planetary ministry of social, biological, and spiritual uplift. The monumental work of remaking a world of near-savages and hunters into a veritable paradise of peace-loving horticulturists lie ahead.

Van shouted, "Now to the east, for a look at your estate." Van then pointed his bird toward the Adamic estate. During this glide eastward, Van drew attention to certain features. "Look to the south," he pointed at a large group of housing clusters off to their right on the flat valley plains. "The homes of the workers' families."

Soon Adam and Eve were flying above their future home in Eden's east. "Beautiful!" Eve exclaimed on seeing the layout of their estate with its many housing clusters, and the landscaped pathways between. Large and small trees dotted the estate. The many flowering plants and shrubs shouted out their colors, most of the Garden being near the peak of flowering season.

Eve called out again, "So beautiful!"

After several circles above their soon-to-be home, Van pointed them farther east, to the twelve-gated entrance of the peninsula. They could easily see the two great walls that spanned its neck, a greater inner wall, and a lesser one beyond. Between the two walls, in the center of the peninsular neck, they observed the river that drained the Edenic peninsula. There were six enclosed pathways on each side of the river. Within the boundaries of each park they noted the presence of many beasts. These wild creatures had been moved there to live and serve as a natural line of defense should Eden be attacked from the mainland.

"We are secure!" Adam shouted. "Show us the north."

Van's bird led the way to the north of Eden where they circled over a well-developed area. The Garden dwellers noticed them, shouting out cheers and calling them to come down. They waved but did not land.

"There is the main administrative area," Van shouted. Below were storage facilities for grains and all manner of gardening needs—carts, plows, and wagons, and a dozen pens for work animals. They saw an equal number of shelters and stables for these animal helpers. "There are two medical units, and four guest lodges," he yelled out, pointing toward a group of wooden buildings.

Van sensed Adam and Eve were favorably impressed by what they saw. After circling the area several times, he called out, "Let's tour this area tomorrow." Adam and Eve signaled agreement.

Van then turned the flock, flying south, eventually setting down on the ceremonial mount where the pair had received official welcome two days before.

When they dismounted, Van said, "Amadon and I were hoping you would agree to host a banquet this evening. The Garden workers and their families are curious to see, hear, and come to know you informally."

"Eve and I discussed this last night. You have anticipated our wishes," said Adam.

Amadon told them, "Good then. Preparations have already begun. I had the workers collect three wagonloads of foodstuffs and bring them to the temple's kitchen. And I specified that no meat be served at this banquet, in honor of the preference of the hosts. There are some forty helpers ready and awaiting your consent."

"You have it!" the pair said in perfect unison.

Chapter 8

THE BANQUET

It was near noon when they set down on inaugural mount. Several of the banquet volunteers working outside the Father's Temple noticed the six birds landing and called out to the others. Most stopped their labors and ran to greet Adam and Eve. As they approached, Van and Amadon excused themselves for a meeting with banquet planners.

Adam and Eve met the small crowd then led a joyful procession back to the Father's Temple, gathering more revelers as they went. The spirit of celebration was in them and had been for days.

On arriving at the temple Adam asked for everyone's attention, then said with obvious joy, "Greetings volunteers! The time for celebration is tonight, and our guests are even now gathering. Eve and I are here to help with preparations. Supervisors, join us for a brief planning session." All cheered and went back to their appointed chores singing and enjoying the anticipation of celebration.

Eve gave instructions to the group leaders about timing and dining arrangements. She and Adam then surveyed foods being prepared, offering advice and expressing their preferences. Eve noticed Amadon was leaving with a group of workers. "Where is Amadon going?"

Lyla replied, "He was told very many more guests from outside were expected. He's concerned there isn't enough food. He took twenty workers and four wagons to the fields."

"It appears all is well in hand," said Adam. "Eve and I want to greet as many as we can before the feast. We will remain in the temple area if you need us."

Lyla replied, "There is much to do before evening."

Eve asked, "Do you have the help you need?"

"We have more than enough!" Lam replied. "We had so many volunteers that Amadon created a group in waiting."

Eve then asked, "What are the plans for music?"

"We know only that Van has it planned," Lyla replied.

The pair went to the temple courtyard where the early-arriving banqueters were gathering. Until time to serve, they met and spoke with scores of Garden dwellers and many guests from the mainland villages. All that afternoon various individuals and groups surrounded them, excited and curious well-wishers respectfully listening to the charming, and often profound words that came from the mouths of these celestial newcomers.

When time came to serve their guests, Van called for attention from the central stage saying, "Welcome friends, Garden workers, and guests. The Father of all rules the Earth through his sons and daughters. Other of God's children, the Most Highs, direct them.

"Our wise rulers, abiding in the heavens above, selected these two from the chain of trained ministers that extends from God's home on Paradise down to you, living here on Earth. You are the final link in a line of beings who may know, love, and worship the God of all.

"Adam and Eve were very recently living on a heavenly world. This is where you will ascend to, if you do not reject God's offer to join the universe family. If you accept the offer, you will certainly visit the estates where the Adamic families reside, where they raise remarkable children, and volunteer to come to worlds like ours. The children of the Earth are at the beginning of a new phase of human progress, to be fostered and guided by these two superhumans from on high.

"We gladly acknowledge our Adam and Eve as fellow servants of God. Tonight, they are also the hosts of this banquet; they will eat and drink with you. And just like you, they want to raise families that bear ever more children for God. The Father of the universe began the first family, creating a Son and a Daughter, the first of all creation. This divine Trinity is composed of co-equal Gods, but God the Father always sits at the head of the family table. This original family, this primary three-fold relationship, is here manifested by the appearance of Adam, Eve, and our heavenly Father. God may be invisible to the human eye, but he is ever present, like a good friend in a crisis.

"Would the First Son's and First Daughter's representatives on Earth please open the festivities!" Eve took Adam's arm and they ascended the stage.

The pair embraced each other in a touching expression of their ageless love, then turned and faced the guests. "For three days you have welcomed us. Now, we would thank you and feast with you on the Garden's bounty," proclaimed Eve. "By your team labors the fields have produced an abundance, an impressive variety of superior foods for Garden residents; and enough to share with our friends outside. Let this banquet foreshadow even more fruitful teamwork, even a Garden that feeds everyone, in every land."

All cheered then fell silent as Adam spoke just as eloquently, words of prayer and thanksgiving: "Father, we offer our humble gratitude for your many gifts, the greatest of these being life and love. There would be no life, no love, no families to cherish—no meaning, no value, and no purpose without you. We thank you for the bounty of things we have, and for the things you have prepared. We will always pray for your help and now, this day, we ask that these fruits of the field receive your blessing. Enliven us and guide us Father, with your wishes, your will, your way, and your wisdom."

Eve spoke these final words before the tables were opened, "Adams and Eves are charged with the responsibility of ruling their planet until its culture can be brought to full spiritual blossom. This will require an age, countless days working together. In all this you should realize our final Father never stops caring for his children, never ceases visiting them in the form of divine teachers and heavenly ambassadors. Take these Garden viands into your bodies. May they, and more like them, provide the strength and health needed to serve God, family, and the Garden, all your days on Earth." She then looked to Van and Amadon.

Amadon shouted, "Let the banquet be served, let the festivities begin!"

Suddenly the air was filled with sounds from musicians playing a joyful melody that immediately heightened the celebratory mood. The music quickly drew the attention of the children playing outside the courtyard and they enthusiastically joined the jubilation and feasting inside. All the musical instruments produced wonderful sounds, remarkable harmonies that were unheard prior to Van and Amadon starting the Garden. Before Adam and Eve came, Garden workers had crafted these advanced instruments under Van's tutelage. The best of the Garden's musicians had been training on them for several decades.

After the introductory music Amadon gave a signal and the musicians began playing a beautiful song that Van and certain talented Garden residents had composed and rehearsed for this occasion. This rhapsody drew everyone's attention, warming hearts and relaxing minds. The diners moved to the overflowing tables, filling their bowls and cups in good spirit. Much gentle laughter and warm conversations harmonized with the beautiful melodies, with the eating, dancing, and singing.

During this festive mix of Garden workers and mainland guests, most all had a chance to meet or at least come close enough to hear Eve or Adam. All the while, the musicians played their tunes. The pair delighted in meeting and conversing with both adults and children that night. And they expressed sincere gratitude for the quality of the music Van and Amadon provided. "An unexpected pleasure," Adam declared.

The festivities finally broke up near dawn. All faces were beaming with the joy of sustained and loving association. Eve and Adam knew the night had been a social success. It provided an excellent beginning for living and working with their human associates, already thousands in number.

As the sun broke over the eastern horizon the pair took a long walk with Lyla and Lam following. Eve said to Adam, "We have many good and willing workers, and an excellent plan."

"Van and Amadon exceeded my expectations," he replied. "Some of the most challenging work is done. Even our home is ready and awaits us."

Eve replied, "After flying over our home-to-be, I am wanting very much to go there, and I would like to invite some of the estate's caretakers' families to reside nearby, until our children are many. And shouldn't we reserve an area for guests of the Garden?"

Adam looked into her eyes and said with some longing, "How I look forward to the day when our houses are filled with family."

"You're missing them too..."

"I am." They stopped and embraced but looked so lonely.

As the sun rose over the fragrant and newly misted Garden, the pair walked and discussed a plan to address the Garden workers later that day, to build on the warmth and friendship of the night before. Midmorning they returned to the Father's Temple as they wished to consult with Van and Amadon on certain details of their address.

Chapter 9

FOURTH DAY

While Adam, Eve, Van, and Amadon made final adjustments to the address, the children of banquet guests were already up and playing as their parents slept on. It was mid-morning when all four were fully satisfied with its content and wording.

Van said, "Amadon and I will, if you are in agreement, broadcast word that everyone should gather at inaugural mount, midafternoon, for this final address before we resume work under your administration." They agreed and parted, later to meet on the mount.

Eve then went, for the first time, to the Tree of Life and filled a large basket with its ripe fruits. As she was about to turn and leave with Adam, an angel, the "Voice of the Garden," spoke saying, "Should good and evil be combined, the Adamic Son and Daughter will become as mortals." And for the next 117 years, every time Eve or Adam collected fruit and leaves from the tree, the Garden's Voice, that angel, one named Solonia, spoke those same words of warning.

She and Adam then retreated to their little cottage for a short rest and sustenance before the afternoon meeting. Lyla and Lam made certain they weren't disturbed. After their second meal on Earth and a brief respite, the four walked to the mount where Adam and Eve would speak to the Garden staff once again, this time about the future of Eden.

The faces of last night's banqueters were still aglow with celebratory friendliness and the sheer joy of being in the Garden near the divinely lovely Adam and Eve. From their hilltop view the pair was pleased to see the shiny faces of workers and supervisors now eager to hear and follow them.

Adam began, speaking with tremendous sincerity; "Eve and I have made plans for a gradual but definite path to the first age of Light and Life. Van has informed you that this is the goal of all evolving planets. Most of you know the Earth's previous administration also had plans. But it is sorrowful indeed that those plans were not followed, and that a sinful rebellion occurred.

"It was a setback in time but it provided precious wisdom we may now reflect upon, and thereby, avoid another such incident. Almost all the gains of 300,000 years were lost when the original plan was abandoned in favor of one that rejected our Heavenly Father's rulership and attempted to shortcut the proven path to perfection.

"But when that wicked plan failed, God did not retire in defeat and humiliation. Our Paradise Father is tireless and undefeatable. Truth and goodness will always win; will always triumph, even if there are obstacles, delays, and betrayals.

"Even if a son from on high, a being entrusted with the watch-care of a whole world, does turn his administration against God, all is not lost. Our Father, in wisdom and righteousness, simply sets that son aside and sends another more trustworthy son or daughter, one who will take up the assigned mission without diverting the divine plan and plunging the world into chaos. One who will reestablish order and redirect the misguided world toward its rightful and intended destiny.

"How can we accomplish all this you may ask? Eve and I will ever answer, 'One small step at a time, never ceasing.'"

Eve then said, "The first step is to complete the Garden.

That alone will require many generations and much more of your good labors. While the Garden is being developed, while its social and spiritual culture is being advanced, the next step will be unfolding.

"Simultaneous with the Garden's development, Adam and I will bear much fruit from our bodies, producing many children. Just as the Garden feeds and enlivens us, we will someday feed the world with new life that took origin here. When the number of our children is great, they will offer themselves as biological contributors to that of humanity's evolved biology.

"And all along we will labor to more firmly establish the government of God on the Earth. Then, on some far-distant day, the first buds of the flower of Light and Life will emerge— a great spiritual age will begin, one in which God and humans cooperate, harmonize, and co-create a transcendent civilization that reaches every family, no matter how remote, no matter how backward."

Eve went on, "But that day is indeed far away. Many of you will live a full life here in the Garden and yet see little of the divine plan come to fruition. But know this: When your service has been rendered, when your body has run its course on the Earth, it will die. But *you* will resurrect on a better world, a world of unimagined beauty and divine grandeur.

"Sooner or later you will arrive at the original Garden of Eden on Edentia, where there exists such botanical perfection that it has become the model, the pattern, for the Gardens of a thousand worlds.

"So, you have been informed that when your body dies, you will live on. Your essence, your soul, will go to the worlds from which we so recently departed. There you will take up life anew, in another and more enduring body. We have seen the resurrection of mortals; it is *real* and you will live again.

"The physical bodies that Adam, Van, Amadon, and I possess are not meant to die; they are designed to last as long as we serve the Father and his children here on Earth. The Tree of Life maintains our connection to the spirit-mind energies that nourish us. The fruit of the Tree of Life enables our bodies to absorb this form of energy that is unknown to you.

"Our bodies utilize the energies the tree gathers from the stars, energies created to sustain specially constructed life forms like ours, even indefinitely. But your bodies are designed to wear out in a relatively short time. Physical death is but a doorway to new life elsewhere in Our Father's vast universe, to many other mansions, worlds like and unlike the Earth. Believe me when I tell you there is a world whereon the first Garden of Eden grows, nigh to where the Most Highs abide. Someday, when our work is finished on Earth, we will join you on the ascent to Paradise. If you choose to follow that path do not doubt the Most Highs will welcome you to their matchless Garden.

Adam then said, "Before Eve and I finalized our plans for Earth, we studied the methods and results of other Adamic bestowals on other worlds of our system, some of which were also betrayed by their rulers. And since arriving we have taken further council and received valuable advice from Van, Amadon, and the Melchizedek Receivers."

Their charming voices carried well over the silent crowd. All were keenly listening. Adam continued. With touching sincerity he said, "Although we have somewhat different forms, and we will have longer life spans than you, we are, in our essence, not that different from you.

"We can work together, we can and will complete this great and challenging task. It is an unimaginable future of increasing perfection and divinity attainment that awaits the citizens of the Earth. This is a challenge that will require devotion, assistance, and loyalty from every one of you, from your children, your grandchildren, even thousands of generations to come.

"Untold centuries will be required to achieve the final goal. And this is the reason our bodies were designed as they were; to carry us through tens of thousands of years—hundreds of thousands if necessary—to bring the Earth and all its inhabitants into harmony with divine destiny. It is the goal of all worlds to someday reach an age of Light and Life in which humanity blooms ceaselessly, bearing its very best and most prolific fruit. Life in this Garden may seem like heaven to you. But life in the ages to come will be as if Paradise had come to Earth, to all the Earth and all her children.

"We ask you now, will you fully pledge your life's service, even your families to come, to this mission, to this cause? Loyalty to our mission is essential. There is a tremendous amount of work ahead, and reward. Eve and I are about to begin our assigned work, completing the Garden and creating a half-million-member family. These coming generations of Adamic children will be our children alone. But they will someday leave Eden and take Adamic culture everywhere there are humans, blending the two into one great civilization.

"Eden has a capacity of one million, according to the plans the Melchizedek receivers made before our arrival. Eve, I, and our children, shall create one half that number over the coming centuries, therefore will there be abundant land and housing for you and your families inside the Garden. After reaching that number, the Adamic family will begin sending our children to each nation, on each continent.

"Our family-to-be will someday marry into your families yet unborn. Waves of our future sons and daughters will go out into the world to share and spread Adamic life and culture, eventually to every place and every family on Earth. It will spread until all of humanity has been lifted up and invigorated with new ideas and new endowments, physical, mental, and spiritual. This isn't a plan original with us, or just for the Earth. Every world is so destined. None are forgotten or ignored.

"Perhaps you have noted how I treat Eve as my equal; this relationship will be the model for the planning, creation, and administration of the Garden. Men and women require one another to carry out the Father's plan on Earth. Loving and thoughtful cooperation between couples, families, and nations is essential if we are to bring about an advanced civilization. No world is considered civilized until men and women have developed mutual respect and sympathetic understanding that goes beyond mere self-interest. The relationship between a woman and a man determines the quality of the families they create. And the quality of the family directly determines the quality of civilization. As goes the family so goes the world."

Eve added, "Though it will require thousands of years, when our family has reached one half million in number, we will direct our children to take themselves to the children of the Earth and impart a new living component designed to foster divine ideals and inspire innovative ideas.

"When Adamic blood is blended with that of races living on a world like Earth, when it is spread abroad, a new age is inaugurated. The biological uplift provided by Adams and

Eves triggers rapid evolution in both body and mind. This leads to a place where God's spirit presence can indwell all such advanced minds. Adamic uplift leads and inspires. When quality thinking and acting dominate in the realms of religion, philosophy, art, music, humor, recreation, government, education, and scientific understanding, society is transformed, it verges on a new way of being, even a new way of dying."

She concluded, saying, "When all the world has been invigorated by the violet infusion, when humans have created one religion centered on God, when the world has one government founded in divine principles and ideals, when there is one common language—then will the ages of Light and Life begin dawning on the Earth. One race of humanity can then live in peace, and thereby progress rapidly toward its intended goal. And you, humble workers, will have set the foundation stones for these glorious ages with your tireless service and generous spirit.

"Finally, do not let evil forces deter us or distract us from achieving the Father's good mission. You know, by Van's teachings, of the opposing rebels who roam the Earth intent on mischief, those who work to recruit others for their wicked work. And perhaps you or your kinsmen have seen and experienced troubles created by these disobedient ones lurking behind the veil of invisibility, those who would have us fail. Do not doubt that the Father is with us, and that our Father never fails. In their missions, daughters and sons may pervert the divine plan, as did our predecessors. But we shall not. We intend, with your help, your support, your loyal service and devotion, to advance Our Father's plan on the Earth, even though numerous obstacles surely await."

Adam and Eve gestured toward Van to close the address: "My friends, tomorrow we begin in earnest! Rejoice and revel for the remainder of the day, for tomorrow we return to our labors. When we take up our work again, let it be done in the spirit of the Father who loves not only the world, but also every individual in it. Come now with us to the Father's Temple to honor and worship the God of Heaven who sends his ambassadors to serve the children of the Earth."

The pair descended the mount, leading the assembled group to the temple. As they walked Adam asked Van, "What of tomorrow? We meet the supervisory staff, and them alone?"

Van replied, "The meeting is set. All the Garden's administrative staff is expected to attend, and all are keenly anticipating meeting you. Amadon made the preparations."

"Well done!" Eve said. "Our reception and all that has followed, so far at least, could not have been carried out better."

All filed into the temple's central courtyard where enchanting music filled the air. Van led a touching worship employing very few words.

Chapter 10

FIFTH DAY

On this morning, Adam and Eve, Lyla and Lam, flew north to join Van and Amadon for a day of discussions with the leaders and administrators of the Garden. The day before, Amadon had given instructions to his lieutenants to assemble the Garden's leaders, from the highest to the lowest, in the administrative center, where most lived and worked.

All senior administrators had been appointed and trained by Van and Amadon. Unequivocal support and unquestioning loyalty were required of these leaders. In speaking with them, Adam and Eve went into considerable detail, posing and taking questions, at the same time drawing closer to these humans in friendship, and in the spirit of harmonious teamwork.

"Welcome!" called out Zol, Chief of Garden Administrators, as the transport birds landed. Van and Amadon had arrived earlier. They stood at Zol's side in front of a host of Garden managers and their assistants.

All watched in stunned fascination as their new rulers dismounted. Van prodded Zol who gathered his wits and approached the pair uttering nervously, "I am Zol. Again I say, welcome, to our new friends... Our leaders... Our... Uh... Forgive me. Perhaps you would like to view the headquarters? Or would you prefer to walk the grounds first?"

Adam and Eve smiled at Zol and the assembled administrators. Adam replied, "Greetings chief. Eve and I were impressed by the view from above, by the organization on the ground and by the many well-built structures already in place.

You've made a superb beginning for us. Van told Eve and I about the four generations of administrators and laborers who do the important work of planning, building, and maintaining this beautiful Garden that we are now quite pleased to call home. We congratulate you."

Zol replied humbly, "It is by Van's hand that we plan, move, and do."

Then Eve said to everyone in her charming way, "We would like very much to walk the grounds, have chief Zol tell us of things done and things needing to be done. But first, we would see your headquarters."

Zol commented with the utmost deference, "We like to think of them now, as *your* headquarters, and us as your willing servants." All who heard this voiced strong agreement.

Adam said, "We are humbled that such able and intelligent friends as yourselves are willing to assist us in upbuilding the Garden and leading our primary work: Trade, labor, and education. Until now Van has directed you in these three arenas, inside and outside the Garden. We would not change that direction. Let commerce, Garden improvement, and schooling remain the focus of the Garden's supervisors, for now."

The rest of the day was devoted to discussions of certain governing rules and coming to know the senior leaders, some of whom they had met briefly at the banquet. In the years before Adam and Eve arrived, Van had selected and placed these men and women in their positions, on a temporary basis pending Adam and Eve's approval.

When the group reached the headquarters, Adam told everyone, among other things, that, "Neither Eve nor I intend to make changes in the administrative staff that Van has put in place, other than making your positions permanent." All heartily cheered this decision. It was dawning on Eve and Adam how much these volunteers enjoyed living in and leading the work of the Garden.

The chief led the pair on an extended tour of the central complex of buildings that made up the administrative headquarters, with an entourage numbering in the hundreds following close behind.

Around noon the group assembled in the largest meeting room of the headquarters. Eve opened this meeting of leaders, reiterating what Adam had said: "We will not make changes to the Garden's governance at this time. Van tells us it is functioning smoothly. If, and when, we make changes, they will be gradual, incremental, and experimental. We do not wish to create turmoil or foster confusion by making rapid or arbitrary changes in either leadership or methods.

"We will make ourselves personally available to you at frequent meetings. Your presence will be required at each meeting. Only effective communication and closely coordinated teamwork will bring success in the mission we are undertaking. Van tells us attendance is generally good, we would like for it to be as perfect as possible.

"Between meetings you should communicate with us through your managers and supervisors. They will pass messages up the line to the level of appropriate action. You will find these lines always open between meetings. Work with your superiors, and trust that the chain of command will respond as quickly as possible with the action required. Your chiefs will be the gatekeepers of information and requests when you cannot speak with us directly.

"Because your decisions and efforts are vital to the Garden's core functions and its continuity, governance must be effective, adaptable, far-seeing, and evenly applied. We will rely on you to report when it is not."

Adam told them, "Eve and I are instructing you to continue working with Van and Amadon, as you and your parents have for four generations. But those two steadfast leaders will leave the Earth in due time. Between now and then we shall gradually assume their roles and authority. We have consulted Van about modifying administrative methods. He and the Melchizedek Council both suggest very gradual implementation of any new directions or plans. Since you are at the level of implementation, we will rely on your observations before, during, and after changes or modifications.

"Eve and I have been informed there are mischief-makers in the ranks of the workers. We were told you administrators are aware of this and have been, as best you can, dealing with those who want to delay or divert the Garden's master plan.

"You may be certain Eve and I will be vigilant to fend off their trouble. Be ever wary of these influences, they can be deceptively subtle and tragically consequential. But do not expel any rebellious workers from the Garden, neither should you promote them. It is better that they are here to see and taste the fruits of our combined labors. They may, someday, be persuaded to commit wholly to our plan for world transformation, or at least the Garden's."

Adam later said this meeting immensely strengthened their budding relationship with these experienced leaders. The pair's personal interactions fostered an abiding trust with most of the Garden administrators. Simply stated, they were enamored by the couple's charming behavior and modest demeanor, having now observed them here, at the banquet, and at their welcoming. Almost everyone discerned and enjoyed the spiritual flavor exuded by these handsome, violet-skinned beings from on high.

Eve then struck a serious tone. "Adam and I are putting our trust in your wise decisions and good labors so that our mission may come to full fruition. As the pace of progress picks up, you leaders of the Garden will ever be confronted with additional responsibilities and new challenges. And we will ever be available as your leaders, counselors, and friends.

"The Garden's master plan has many parts," Eve said. "Some are already in place, as with the outposts on the mainland. Good relations with the tribes outside assure future trade and cultural exchange.

"So you have some idea of our broader plan, know that we will create an *Edenic League*. This league is intended to nurture the ideals of representative government. Such a model organization will, eventually, inspire responsible, wise, and efficient self-governance. These goals may seem strange and even dangerous to this generation, but do not doubt that they will become the standard for peoples that come to respect and enjoy such freedoms."

Adam revealed more, saying, "Leaders assigned to the Edenic League will be charged with establishing superior manufacturing systems inside and outside the Garden. We will create new and useful commodities to foster trade relations with neighbors. There is no greater peace-maker than mutually beneficial trade. And there is no better way to export the Edenic culture than by producing desirable goods bearing the mark of the Garden. The League will require a well-trained corps of laborers, craftsmen, and ambassadors. Outside trade is a crucial factor of the Garden plan; Eve and I will devote much time and effort expanding the good start you have made in manufacture and trade.

"As you know, Van and Amadon have long been working outside the Garden opening lines of communication and establishing trade. Many of you have helped in this important work. Eve and I have been told the Garden's staff has already befriended many tribal leaders who will, hopefully, develop social and trade centers in their villages.

"Eve and I will work with you, improving the quality of the trade-goods and increasing the number of trader-ambassadors at the Edenic outposts. We will send out social ambassadors and teachers of religion. In these ways, by these methods, we will be spreading more and more seeds of Garden culture, both material and spiritual.

"Tomorrow morning you should resume your roles, the work that Van and Amadon assigned. I would remind you, tell your laborers that changes will always be made in graduated steps and with due consideration. Change requires time, and the greater the change the more time required. Inform the Garden workers in your charge that they may rest assured of our support and steady leadership, as may you.

"And now Eve and I would meet with the senior administrators about immediate steps in improving the Garden's communication system, about better methods of making and preserving work and maintenance records. Van has stated these aspects of Garden organization should be a priority. And they should improve efficiency, reduce errors, and enhance our chances of fruitful teamwork.

"You are our representatives, and as such you are viewed as members of the Garden's governing family, extensions of our family. Your good works shall become a solid foundation of a permanent system of governance led by Eve and me."

Eve ended with an announcement: "Tell your workers, helpers, and families that the next Garden event will be very soon. It will be our honor to administer the marriage vows of volunteers and guests alike. The first to wed will be our personal aides, Lyla and Lam." She pointed to them.

"Inform other couples who have been waiting for our arrival to exchange their oaths. Group weddings will be a frequent occurrence in the Garden, on the evenings of the full moon." Everyone cheered this announcement and soon every couple wanting to marry had enrolled in the event.

Adam and Eve then met with the twelve senior administrators. They heard many of the concerns on the minds of these willing supervisors and eager managers. And they listened closely to their suggestions and advice. After this historic meeting, the leaders went to their homes and places of work, expressing to everyone how impressed they were with Eve's grasp and command of the Garden's labor situation, and her role as an equal half of the Garden's ruling duo. And all were relieved and pleased to hear that no grand or arbitrary changes were coming simply because they miraculously appeared and intended to assert authority.

Chapter 11

SIXTH DAY

Having spent the previous 15,000 years studying and training as experimental biologists in the system's life laboratories, Adam and Eve were intimately familiar with every creature of the Earth, from the greatest to the least. They knew the origin, class, nature, and evolution of every living thing in both the animal and plant kingdom. Before their sojourn on Earth, they were regarded as two of the most expert anatomists in the entire system.

The sixth day was another day of flying over Eden's lush valley. First eastward to the double security walls that protected the peninsula from the mainland. They circled over the twelve-section park that separated the inner from the outer wall, observing the variety and approximate number of beasts that roamed within.

The pair and their flying entourage touched down in several places inside the Garden during this morning, to mingle with surprised and adoring workers. All were astounded by their seemingly inexhaustible knowledge of plants and animals. At one point they spoke about living creatures too small to be seen. Often, they compared Earth creatures with those inhabiting other worlds. Word quickly spread about the astonishing knowledge of plant and creature life both Eve and Adam possessed.

At another touch-down in their Garden tour, Eve said to a large group working on the cistern system, "Van has rightly taught you that certain tiny creatures will do harm should they enter the drinking water and your bodies. But others of them are helpful in preparing and preserving the soil. Yet other invisible organisms live inside your bodies and are essential for health maintenance."

Those who listened to Adam and Eve that morning told others about their encyclopedic knowledge of living creatures. These reports became rumors that were exaggerated or embellished. That added to a growing reverence for the couple.

After the morning tour they took flight and set down briefly at the Father's Temple, to the delight of workers who were tending the temple grounds. After a short visit with the groundskeepers they decided, rather than going to the cottage to eat, they would join the temple's kitchen staff who were about to sit for a meal when the pair arrived unannounced. Before sitting Eve went to the tree and selected fruit and leaves to supplement their food. And once more she heard Solonia's admonition about mixing good and evil.

That afternoon the six flew west to dedicate the Garden's new campus. Very soon after this visit the first phase of construction was completed and Eden's schools for children of residents and guests opened its doors. The Garden plan provided that the Adamic children would also attend the western academy, but only after completing their primary education in the schools of east Eden near the Adamic home.

The fandors carrying Adam, Eve, Van, Amadon, Lyla and Lam, landed on a hilltop near the center of the future school. Already had Amadon and his work crews begun landscaping the grounds.

In preparation for this meeting, Van had prearranged a speaker. The candidate dean of the schools, a distinguished woman named Laotta, welcomed the group. She was a brilliant and capable Nodite woman who Van and Amadon had chosen from a host of volunteers. She was already a renowned teacher among the Nodites. Later that day Eve and Adam confirmed her as dean.

Workers stopped and gathered when they saw the six land. Laotta led Adam and Eve to a modest platform that had been specially built for this address. Laotta stepped forward saying in a commanding voice. "Greetings all. The future directors and staff of the western schools of Eden delight in welcoming our new leaders from on high. Van taught us much about you, but nothing could match the pleasure of an actual meeting. We are honored by your presence, and I do here and now fully pledge our continuing cooperation in the education and training of the Garden's youth. And, with your consent, guests will be permitted to attend, learn, and then take this acquired knowledge back to their villages.

"In doing all this, we will ever be loyal to you, our new leaders. We shall not falter in assisting you to recapture God's righteous rule on our now quarantined world.

"It is the intention of the board of directors that this school shall become an extension of the Adamic mission and cause. Our plan is to foster a new and lasting culture in your name, one founded on the divine ideals and personal values that Van has so long taught, and so long exemplified. Upon that foundation your sovereign rule will begin—and stand for many millennia.

"With your permission, it shall be the policy of Eden and its schools that all who are sincere in pursuit of knowledge and truth, shall be admitted. I may be the candidate dean of the schools, but in fact you, Adam and Eve, are its true leaders. You are my superiors to whom the directors and I pledge lifelong loyalty.

"And now, it is only fitting that the new masters of the Garden, and eventually the Earth, be permitted to bless this ground, the schools we are building here, and the fruits of enlightenment soon to come."

Adam stood to thank Laotta, "Eve and I are indebted to every Garden worker. Raising a family is the only endeavor more important than schools. Indeed, the two are intimately intertwined and mutually beneficial. Van tells me you have a curriculum?"

"We do!" Laotta exclaimed. "May I offer an overview?"

Eve encouraged her, "Please, yes!"

Laotta proceeded, "Of course the general education plan for our school, one created by Van and Amadon, can and will be amended according to your wishes. Their plan is divided by age. Classes and activities for the younger students will change twice as often as the older. And, on reaching age sixteen, your children, educated in the east of Eden will be invited to come west to teach our children. And here they may obtain advanced and specialized education.

"The primary goal of the schools of the west is socialization. This will be taught each day in three ways:

1. Mornings will be used to instruct students in the methods and art of agriculture. Team projects will simultaneously teach gardening and promote cooperation.

2. Afternoon periods will be devoted to games for the exercise of body and mind, in which students play competitively.

3. Evenings will be used to form and enhance friendships, fostered by social activities designed for that purpose.

"It will be the responsibility of the family to instruct children in the matters of spirituality and personal intimacy. Parents will have access to special classes to learn how best to impart the morality and ethics of these essential and personal subjects.

"Other themes proposed for the school system of the west, which Van already tested in his schools, prior to your coming, are:

1. Physical maintenance. Nutrition and healing.

2. Ethical behavior.

3. Individual versus community needs.

4. Earth history.

5. Trade relations.

6. Balancing duty and desire.

7. Play and humor.

"History will be taught as Van revealed it: An original pair of human beings evolved one million years ago from the biological formula the Life Carriers implanted more than one half-billion years before.

"This original brother and sister became parents and grandparents many times over. Then, about five hundred thousand years ago, the mother of one family gave birth to the six races of color: red, yellow, blue, green, orange, and indigo. The six races mixed, battled, and migrated across the Earth. The scattered remnants of all those struggles, the surviving stocks of humanity, are destined to blend with the violet race and the Nodite lineage carried in my own blood. After many an age, all the races will be blended, thereby producing an olive shade of human, a mixed heritage vastly more able and creative than the original pair of humans (whom, Van has revealed, were named Andon and Fonta).

"The emergence of the colored races occurred about the same time the Planetary Prince arrived. This was the Earth's first superhuman leader and teacher, number one in a series. For 300,000 years the Prince and his staff followed the divine plan for the Earth: the gradual enlightenment of humanity, the steady refinement of the races, and the eventual uplift of all cultures. The people of the Earth progressed and prospered. But then the Prince joined the system rebellion, instigated by Lucifer, which disrupted progress on thirty-seven worlds, including the Earth. Many angels and midwayers were lost to the rebel's deception. Not long after the outbreak, the worlds in rebellion were all quarantined. And to this day the Earth remains in isolation.

"Van has always taught his students that the appointed Son, the Prince, defaulted. He broke his oath and denounced the divine plan, pledging loyalty to Lucifer and his rebels.

"For over a hundred and sixty thousand years has the Earth drifted and languished in the confusing consequences of administrative betrayal. Such things can happen because free will is freely given. The ways of God may seem strange to we mortals, but the reign of truth, beauty, and goodness, in the individual, and in the collective, is always triumphant, on all worlds. This is accomplished by successive bestowals of divine children. Default or not, truth is always the victor.

"Now, new leadership and new blood have come! We are fortunate to witness the beginning of the second revelation of divine truth on Earth. The faithless, rebel Prince has been cast off. The Most Highs have noted our need and sent other, and worthier, ones to take his place. Even improve our bodies and minds, that we may someday partake of the divine gifts that await the children of the Earth. Adam and Eve are now with us! As Van has so often reminded his students, 'The Gods have not forgotten nor abandoned us!'

"Our students will learn that one of the primary purposes of an Adamic bestowal is to convert humanity from hunters to gardeners. We will also teach the bestowal of an Adam and Eve on a world means they will someday become that world's sovereign rulers, not only the Garden's.

"Van has informed us that you will grow the Adamic family to one half million before mixing your family with the human family. As you build this biological reserve our descendants will continue the construction and beautification of the Garden. It is expected to become a world center of spiritual realization and enlightened philosophy, of scientific achievement, as well as a global marketplace for the exchange of superior goods and ideas.

"And the western schools will bring in exceptional children and adults from outside Eden, so they may begin enjoying the benefits of an inspired educational system. Inviting visitors to attend Garden schools has always improved relations with our neighbors, near and far. I expect, with the inauguration of the western school, even greater improvements will result. By this method, simultaneous advancement unfolds in Garden and world cultures.

"Balanced children come from good families led by wise parents. The schools of the west will teach that a two-parent, mother-father family is the ideal. Children require both parents and a loving home to manifest their greatest potential throughout life. Adam and Eve descended to Earth to provide a divine model for the ideal family. We are honored and pleased to have them here as models, teachers and friends.

"Welcome Eve and Adam! Welcome attending angels! The Garden now has its full complement to begin your rule. Van's prediction and its fulfillment have energized every member of the Garden's schools. Van's educational system, its administrators and teachers, are now put at your command." Laotta pointed to a group of her teaching associates, and then invited the pair to speak.

"Thank you, Laotta," said Eve, "the school is indeed fortunate to have such a brilliant teacher. Adam and I do heartily support your candidacy as dean of the western schools. Your grasp of this world's history and the scope of our mission is commendable. Once more, we see how well Van has prepared the way. We offer our blessing, our encouragement and cooperation, for your good works in the education and socialization of the Gardens' most important product, our children."

Adam then prayed, "Heavenly Father, guide us as we attempt to bring your good blessings to all who would come to this place of learning. May they leave it better, wiser, and with a greater understanding of you and your righteous purpose. You are our beacon and our destiny, even the Great Teacher in the vast school that is the universe."

The rest of the afternoon was spent fraternizing with Laotta and the men and women who were going to staff the school. The pair spoke with many of these teachers, offering gratitude and advice, along with prayers and promises of support.

Before sunset, the six bade Laotta and the school's staff Godspeed in their educational endeavors. Eve said to them, "The two schools, east and west, must be coordinate partners. Adam and I will arrange regular meetings to insure both schools teach the same facts, and the same truths."

Laotta and her staff were deeply impressed by this visit. They were charmed by the pair, and pleased that these new managers approved Laotta as dean. It is noteworthy that Laotta's granddaughter became well known later on, but not as a teacher.

As they were about to depart to spend the first night in their permanent home, Adam took Van aside and said, "Spread the message… tell everyone in the Garden that tomorrow shall be a day of rest. Eve and I are very much looking forward to time at home without plans or obligations. We would have the Garden workers and their families do the same."

Van replied, "The word shall be broadcast. You shall have your well-earned rest in your new abode. Amadon will go with you and set a guard around it."

Adam asked, "Is there danger there? I would prefer that we not insulate or isolate ourselves at home."

Eve said, "Perhaps this first night, it would be wise."

The six then flew east. Van wished them good night as he dropped down at the Father's Temple to announce the day of rest. Adam and Eve were keenly anticipating a full day's leisure after the previous six days of intense socializing, planning, and adjusting.

It was about sunset when the five set down at the fandor stable in the east of Eden. There were almost two hundred residents and staff anxiously expecting their arrival, having just heard of it by a messenger pigeon Amadon had dispatched before leaving the west. On landing the pair spoke a few words of gratitude and appreciation to their adoring welcomers, giving a promise to speak more, after they had rested.

The eldest staff member and directing manager of the estate led them to Adam and Eve's permanent residence. As they entered she told them, "We hope you will be at home and at ease here. Van showed us how to build your residence, but he said you would like to decorate it. So, we provided only these things."

Baskets, quilts, and other household items had been placed along one wall. "It is just as I had hoped," said Eve. Adam indicated agreement with a broad smile. Lyla and Lam surveyed the house, inspecting each room.

The elder left, bidding them good rest and requesting they attend a dinner in their honor the following week, hosted by the estate's caretakers, gardeners, and their children. The invitation was quickly accepted, and with sincere gratitude.

Before Amadon left to arrange the guards' schedule, he, Eve, and Adam very briefly discussed the eighth day's schedule and duties. When Amadon departed, all four went immediately to their beds, disrobing and hardly speaking a word before falling soundly asleep.

Chapter 12

SEVENTH DAY

This day, intended to be a day of rest for Adam and Eve, at least one without formal activities, was also supposed to be a time of settling into their new home. Instead it began before dawn with an alarming message.

While the four lay resting, a midwayer delivered an urgent request to Amadon, who went immediately to Adam and Eve's front door, calling out, "It is unfortunate I must wake you. Van has summoned you to the temple, without delay." Lyla and Lam were awakened and heard this message.

The pair came out and Eve asked, "What is the *matter*, Amadon?"

"The message given was only that you should come," he replied. Lam and Lyla, standing in their room's doorway, looked at each other knowingly.

Adam noted their expression and asked, "What could have happened?" Lyla said, "At our meal yesterday in the Father's Temple, we heard some of the workers, ones who met you earlier and heard your teachings about every animal and plant... they were so impressed that they wanted to do something. There was talk of a meeting by the Father's Temple."

Amadon said, "I ordered your flyers be readied."

Van had sent his message as events were unfolding. For hours, on the temple grounds under the soft light of a waning moon, certain leaders and their followers had been lighting and fanning flames of adoration. They stoked this fire of adulation in the minds and hearts of hundreds of Garden residents, and not a few guests.

Lyla was told later that one of the more devout leaders spoke passionately and convincingly to a large group of enraptured listeners and would-be worshippers. He declared that, "Adam and Eve are from God, and of God. And we should honor them as gods!"

He and others went on building up enthusiasm and reverence until the growing consensus tipped the balance to call for all-out worship of the newly arrived son and daughter of God. Since Adam and Eve were far away in the east of Eden, they turned to Van who was struggling vainly to quell this misplaced urge to venerate.

Van objected saying, "Adam and Eve are a son and a daughter of God, as am I, as are you! They are pledged to become the helpmates of the Earth… but they are not gods. God may have sent them, but they too worship him. We are all to worship this same God whose children we all are."

But none would listen to one who might himself be divine. Someone called out, "How is it you live 1600 centuries without decay or age? And wasn't your origin also in heaven? Did you not predict the coming of this son and daughter? And all these years, did you not direct us in creating a Garden to receive them as if they are gods? You too must be a god!"

Van escaped just before the revelers could seize and carry him to the inaugural mount to become the object of their worship. On leaving the clamor Van summoned the midwayers.

Midwayers are marvelously adept, having many superhuman skills. This little known and unique order of being acquired that name because they are mid-way between humans and angels. They have strengths and abilities far superior to humans—and some the angels do not. If midwayers need to transport a material being through the air, that too is possible.

Like the angels, midwayers are invisible to human eyes. And, like the angels, they can defy gravity. They have the ability to move about the planet with lightning speed. They neither eat nor drink as does a human. Their energy comes from a source unknown to humanity. Their origin, history, and destiny make a remarkable story by itself.

Midwayers are invaluable to planetary administrators as the invisible agents who form a living bridge between mortal and celestial life. Midwayers are permanent residents of the Earth, and that makes them indispensable as information gatherers. They provide accurate facts and continual updates on the world's inhabitants to the planet's supervisors and angelic ministers. They do not die; they live on and become a living repository of the history and daily events of the world. And they will become very useful to Adam and Eve later on... as they were that night to Van.

Van once told Lam and Lyla, "The midwayers are essential links in the chain of beings from the Father on Paradise to humans on Earth. Certain types of midwayers are already present, having been created during the previous planetary administration wherein I originally served.

"We highly value their unique skills as living links between angels and humans. Often, when the angels need something done in the physical realm, they can rely on the midwayers to actually perform the task. They share the angels' ability to move with tremendous speed anywhere on the Earth, and therefore, they can provide vital details to the world's leaders about current conditions everywhere—physical, intellectual, and spiritual. They have the power, should they wish to exercise it, to leave the planet without angelic transport, but they do not. The Earth is *their* home world."

Adam later told Lyla and Lam, "There are thousands of midwayers on the Earth, good and highly skilled beings. And there are many great minds among them. Midwayers are indispensable to our mission. Assigned to Eve and me, are 100,000 ministering angels; they and the corps of loyal midwayers are irreplaceable assistants for the execution and completion of our mission. Midwayers remain on the planet of their assignment assisting each succeeding administration until the ages of Light and Life, until their world is securely rooted in the firmament of Spirit.

"Someday the age-long tasks of Earth's midwayers will be finished, and they too shall ascend to the mansion worlds and eventually to Paradise, alongside mortal sons and daughters who live but an instant of time on Earth before graduating to the heavenly spheres."

Chapter 13

THE CRISIS

Van could see midwayers and communicate telepathically with them. After the close escape he called upon their chief to bring Adam and Eve to the Father's Temple by midwayer transport, to calm and teach the emboldened throng in proper worship.

The vocal leaders were entirely sincere but causing a growing uproar. Workers and supervisors were all but demanding that these visible gods come so they might express this overflow of worshipful feeling that had been growing since the pair's arrival.

So it was early on the morning of the seventh day when the midwayers flashed into action and snatched Adam and Eve from the backs of the fandors just after they had taken flight. They were carried directly and quickly to the center of the trouble. The workers were stunned into silence when Adam and Eve appeared to land without birds or other visible support, their eyes not attuned to the midwayers obediently and carefully transporting them. This was construed as further evidence that they were indeed gods sent down from heaven.

As the pair landed one of the most vocal leaders yelled, "Our gods have come! They can fly!" All the would-be worshipers turned to see. A great roaring cheer went up as the crowd gathered to bow before them.

Adam and Eve assessed the troubling situation as the group encroached. Then both raised a hand to quiet the fervor. After a moment of silence in recognition of Adam and Eve's God-given authority, and in anticipation of any command from the pair, the worshipers looked at them longingly. They fervently hoped one or both would indulge their fiery, soul-felt urge to venerate and worship these newly arrived, and instantly adopted, gods.

Adam then said with the authority of a true leader, "Come, follow us to inaugural mount where Eve and I would speak with you about the object and practice of worship." The beautiful pair promptly led the way on foot, closely followed by these exuberant souls seeking to satisfy an innate, but misdirected, need to give affection and receive divine blessing.

When the raucous crowd was assembled around the inaugural mount, Adam and Eve looked out upon their adoring faces. Adam spoke again in clear and measured voice, "Today is the seventh day of our sojourn on Earth. Eve and I had planned that it be a day of rest. But now we are declaring that it shall be a day of rest *and* worship. Today we will teach you the way of true worship, our method of approaching the only one who deserves such veneration and adoration."

Eve said to them, "You may bestow any respect or honor on us, but never worship. We are our Father's sons and daughters, as are you. We took origin only slightly higher than you. We adore and worship not each other, but the Universal Father who, with limitless righteousness and infinite power, creates all the creatures of heaven and Earth."

"But you are like God!" a woman yelled out.

Adam replied immediately, "We *are* like God, for we are all created in his spirit likeness, but Eve and I are not the Creator and Upholder of the Universe any more than you. And have you not noticed that everyday each of you becomes a bit more god-like? To achieve the perfection of God is the eternal goal, to become Godlike, but never God. No, we are not gods."

Another of the throng shouted, "But we can see you, and you fly without wings! You are gods to us!!" Of course, when she said that a great and sustained chorus of agreement sounded.

Eve responded authoritatively when the cheering subsided, "It is true our Father is not in front of your eyes as we are, but his works are everywhere, even the Earth you now stand upon, and the stars above which are homes to other ascending souls. We did not create this world and the stars. We are fellow creatures who are enjoined by the angels to worship the Father of All—one who graciously and generously bestows all favors that spirit-children have the capacity to receive. Increased spiritual capacity, joy, and creativity are the fruits of genuine worship. This is true, personally and collectively.

"The divine plan of mortal advancement insures evolving civilization will receive every one of God's intended gifts. These bestowals of heaven are kept safe for a time when the individual and the group are able to recognize their value and significance.

"Adam and I come bearing a three-fold gift of physical, intellectual, and spiritual invigoration. But we represent just one of many orders of sonship. Other sons will come to the Earth after us, each bearing a greater gift for the uplift of humanity, and the expansion of the power and influence of sincere, intelligent worship. Worship can be misleading when our Heavenly Father is not its object. Worshipping lesser beings, imperfect beings, can only lead to disappointment and division.

"With us, a new era begins in the administration and evolution of world affairs, but there is a Maker who sets up the worlds," said Eve emphatically. "Our God is the one to worship, the one all who *know* worship."

The questions and answers went on until the sun was high. Eve and Adam succeeded in convincing almost everyone that God alone was to be the recipient of worship, not them or Van.

It was a momentous day. Just before noon Adam and Eve ceased their impromptu lecture. Adam pointed to the Father's Temple saying: "Now we will lead you to the material emblem of the Father's invisible presence on Earth, to his temple that sits at the center of the Garden. Let us there bow down in worship of him who made us, and who watches over every living being until our Earth days are done. And let this act of worship also become a sincere pledge that you will never again be tempted to worship anyone but God, our Father and Creator."

Eve concluded this touching exchange between leaders and listeners saying, "Follow us now, to the Father's Temple that we may give all due and proper worship to the one who is most deserving."

And this was the origin of the seventh day being devoted to worshipful contact with the Maker of the Universe, and he alone. From that day forward, workers, administrators, guests, Adam and Eve, all gathered at the Father's Temple at noon on the seventh day for group worship.

The Sabbath day tradition originated this way, thanks largely to the timing of Adam and Eve's over-awing lectures on plant and animal life on the sixth day. The Garden volunteers meant well, and Adam and Eve found a way to turn their good intentions into a weekly habit of worship and progressive spiritual development.

This seventh day was originally dedicated only to worship and rest. Gradually it took on certain other traditions somewhat reflective of the daily routine of Eden's schools. It evolved that, before noontime worship, attention was given to physical activity. After the worship period, instruction regarding the quality of thinking was given. The evening of this seventh day was usually spent freely socializing, rejoicing in friendships and the family feelings that come from such intimate associations and habitual practices. This seventh day worship tradition was adopted by all the Garden's temples following the crisis.

Chapter 14

FIRST MONTH

Having established a God-anchored weekly routine, Adam and Eve devised a yearly plan, a ten-year plan, a hundred-year plan, and a thousand-year plan. They built these plans on foundations Van and Amadon had already laid, adapting as circumstances required. And always did circumstances arise, some of them brought about by the enemies of Adam and Eve.

Despite the many looming difficulties, very soon there was joy in the Adamic household. One morning Eve called Lyla and Lam to say, "Adam wants to make an announcement."

Lyla looked hard at Eve and proclaimed, "You're with child!" Lam eyed Eve closely wondering how Lyla knew that.

Adam smiled and said to Lyla, "We noticed you are as well."

"Time to perform marriages Adam," said Eve. "Do you have multiple births in your family line, Lyla?"

"Yes, we both do," Lyla answered.

Word spread around the Garden and over the mainland very fast, that the first child, maybe twins, or even triplets, would be born to Eve and Adam in less than a year. And with this message went an open invitation to Garden workers to be married in the first ceremony performed by Adam and Eve. And so it was, the pair performed marriages for Adamic children, for Garden residents and Garden guests, all during their lifespans, some five hundred years. Almost every couple, living inside or outside the Gardens, wanted to be married by Eve and Adam.

At high noon on the Saturday of their fourth week on Earth, Adam and Eve officiated at their first wedding ceremony. Lyla and Lam stood at the head of the group of twenty-one couples who had been awaiting this moment in joyful anticipation.

In front of the overflow of Garden workers and guests who were assembled at the courtyard surrounding the Father's Temple, Eve opened the ceremony. She began in clarion tones saying, "From this day on, and in this Garden, it shall be our family's honor and privilege to administer the vows of marriage to your families and ours. It is a cherished duty that Adam and I hope to enjoy frequently."

Adam called out, "Bring forth the men and women to be wed! And let these couples be the first in a long, long line of mothers and fathers whose children will share in the service of God whom we all worship, and who himself is the Father of the Universe."

Amadon signaled Lam and Lyla to lead the group to the altar. There they formed a semicircle facing Eve and Adam.

With planetary authority and the charm of a goddess, Eve spoke these words to the forty-two: "Take now the hand of your beloved, and say before the Father of All, and to each other, 'By this vow, on this day, I take you, and no other, unto myself."

All looked in their mates' eyes and repeated, *By this vow, on this day, I take you, and no other, unto myself.*

Adam administered the second vow, "Say now to your mate, 'Let us pledge our two lives as one in service of the family of God our Father.'"

And they vowed: *Let us pledge our two lives as one in service of the family of God our Father.*

Eve recited the third vow, "Say now to the other, 'I do hereby reserve myself to you, and you alone. This we shall teach to our children.'"

I do hereby reserve myself to you, and you alone. This we shall teach to our children.

Adam then offered the final vow, "Say also unto your beloved, 'Let us follow the will of the Father in bringing and rearing our sons and daughters.'"

The couples repeated, *Let us follow the will of the Father in bringing and rearing our sons and daughters.*

Eve finished with these words, "And now, let it be known to all, in every place, the wedlock of these good men and women. In the eyes of our Father, and we of the Earth, they are now as one. Be fruitful and rejoice in the gift of shared creation with God, our infinite and eternal Creator Father."

Van and Amadon then swung into action, cuing and leading the specially arranged music. Van went to the stage to invite Adam and Eve to be the first to dance. They stepped down onto the courtyards' smooth stone floor and astounded all by their gracious movements to the beautifully composed music.

These melodies were in fact created by Adam and Eve for this very occasion before coming to Earth. Van was made aware of this upon their arrival. Most of the instruments needed for this wedding concert had been created under his supervision prior to the pair's arrival. The others were made after, by an artisans group attached to the Garden's administrative offices. This was another of Van's innovations.

The twenty-one couples followed Adam and Eve's lead, stepping forward and imitating their movements, some better than others.

After the celebrations, when all had feasted and danced to body and soul's content, Lam and Lyla approached Eve and Adam to thank them and confess their growing affection, and to express their wish to do even more.

Lam said to the now radiantly beaming Eve and Adam, in the sincerest way he could, "We are very pleased to be chosen as your aides, even being allowed to serve your family. Lyla and I hope we will soon have many children. They can know your children, they can work and play together. But we would know your true wishes. Do you want to have Lyla and I continue to live in your home? Soon you will have a child. We were thinking of making a home, one nearby. That way you and Lyla can remain close. And either of you can call on us at any time."

"Remain with us for now," Eve said. "Until the children begin to fill the house. Adam and I don't want to live alone."

Adam added, "When the children come you may take the abode next to ours. It has room for your family-to-be, and we will still have your good services."

Lyla asked, "Whose baby will come first? I pray it's yours."

With a hearty laugh Adam smiled and said, "Perhaps today's marriages will bring about much competition. I pray so."

It was nearing sunset when Lyla and Lam excused themselves, going to the fandor stable. There other couples were also departing for their abodes, for a period of nuptial consummation and familial bonding. Adam and Eve lingered into the evening, enjoying the company and conversation of the remaining guests.

Thus ended the first month of the Adamic regime. Much progress had been made. Already was the seven-day week established. The weekly day of rest and worship was firmly in place and has remained so to this day. And a monthly holiday was set around the marriage festivities. Most importantly, the first child of Adam and Eve to be born in the Garden, was now growing in Eve's womb.

Chapter 15

ADAMSON

Long had Adam and Eve trained in the methods of the physical, intellectual, and spiritual development of an evolving world. First, they had to begin to prepare the Garden for the reception and maintenance of the half million pure-line children—which they had already initiated. The first-born was delivered near the end of their first year.

"WAAAHHHHHHHH," came the cry from Eve's very healthy child, after drawing his first breath. Adam and Lyla were in attendance.

"What strong voice, that one!" Adam said.

"May my first come as easy as yours," Lyla exclaimed.

"Any day now, Lyla," said Eve, taking her baby boy to her breast. He immediately quieted and began suckling.

"Adamson," said Adam, as he stroked the baby's brow. "Welcome child. You shall be my right arm."

Eve then said, for the ears of Lam and the group of residents waiting outside, "Let the word go out, Adamson is born."

Lam ran around the group and out the front gate, yelling, "A boy child is born to Mother Eve!" and kept repeating this as he ran. Shortly the messenger birds were released, and the entire Garden rejoiced in this much-anticipated event. Nearly every family sent a gift of some kind. Over the following week, their home filled with them.

A Garden-wide celebration followed shortly thereafter, at the Father's Temple, in which Adam held the child up before the gathered celebrants saying, "Behold, my beloved brought forth a son!"

Eve then took the child in her arms and said, "He shall be known as Adamson. This is but the first leaf on a vast family tree that will grow to fill our Garden home. When our family size attains the numbers prescribed by Eden's master plan, the sons and daughters of the house of Adam will begin to mate with the sons and daughters of the Earth."

Adam then spoke of his and Eve's near-term goals, saying, "When Material Sons and Daughters appear on an evolving world, we bring a graft of new life. And with it, new mind, by which you may create better tools, finer garments, and improved methods of making everything from drinking vessels to fandor saddles. This we do to improve the quality of your lives, and to establish more and better relations with the world outside the Garden. There are no greater or stronger ties between groups than those involving trade and marriage. Adamson and his future siblings will assist Eve and me in these and other matters."

Eve added, "We plan to establish many more trading posts outside the Garden, to promote good relations with each of the tribes in the region. This is an age-long process, the gradual spreading of Garden culture to all the world. Adamson is the first in a line of Adamic administrators who will work on our behalf, and yours, to advance the mission given us by the Most Highs. Our children will become as hands to Adam and me."

With the assistance of Adam and Eve, Lyla delivered twin girls the following morning. And it was an easy birth. Both babes grew to become story keepers for their generation. Lam named them, Lyla the second, and Lyla the third.

Eve produced five children before the Melchizedek Receivers left, three sons and two daughters. Shortly thereafter her sixth and seventh were born, her first set of twins.

Eve's second and fourth children were female. From the time they were babes, all the Adamic children were taught it was their destiny to mate with their siblings to produce more pure line violet children, up to one-half million.

When their time came, Adamson and Eveson were joined in marriage with their two sisters. They took wedding vows from Adam and Eve alongside Garden dwellers. Many were the marriages the pair performed for their own children. And before long, many were the children playing, laughing, enriching Garden life by their presence.

Chapter 16

DEPARTURE

Day by day, year by year, Van, Amadon, and the Melchizedek Receivers worked ceaselessly to establish the couple as sovereign rulers of the Garden. Always was this accomplished by gradual steps. Van had laid the foundation, now Adam and Eve could build a fully functioning system of permanent governance upon it.

All sixteen worked diligently to transfer leadership and authority to Adam and Eve, knowing full-well that fourteen would soon depart, leaving the pair alone, sole planetary administrators in the midst of enemies and a system-wide rebellion.

One day, after seven years had passed, the chief of the Melchizedek Receivers said to the pair, "Our time with you is short. Van and Amadon are due to ascend. I and my fellow Receivers must soon leave and be about the Father's business on other worlds."

Adam protested vigorously, saying, "Eve and I knew this day would come, but we would request it be postponed. The good counsel we get from you and the other Receivers, the many services provided by Van and Amadon, these are vital and irreplaceable. If the Receivers would consent to just three more years…"

"The decision is made," said the chief kindly but bluntly.

Eve tried to barter, "Even one or two more years would…"

"We Receivers, Van and Amadon, have all agreed the time for our departure is here. Over these seven years the reins of power have been slowly shifted from Van's hands to yours. Know that you are as prepared as you can be to administer the world and its problems, and without us. Have confidence in that. We shall all leave in three days," said the chief in finality.

The farewell ceremony lasted all day, before which Adam and Eve requested repeatedly that departure be postponed. Adam suggested that a pair of Melchizedeks be left in an advisory role, at least until they felt more prepared to assume their roles alone. That too was refused.

Before transporting, the twelve Receivers came to Eve and Adam, one by one, to reassure them. And to offer final bits of advice. By midnight the transport seraphim had taken Van, Amadon, and the twelve Melchizedek Receivers away to Jerusem for continued service on high.

Adam and Eve watched as the Life Carriers dematerialized, and the seraphim enveloped, these fourteen beings. Then they shot off into the night sky.

Gathering her courage, Eve said wistfully, "And now, Adam, Earth is in our watch-care."

"Father, guide us," Adam replied as the last transport seraphim departed with its precious cargo. He fell to one knee, praying, "Father, we would know your will in all things." Eve joined him in praying to know and follow the divine will. But it was so lonely.

Chapter 17

LIFE IN THE GARDEN

Van's original plan for the Adamic estate in the east of Eden was to provide enough housing and other structures to accommodate 300,000 individuals, the center of which was the home of Adam and Eve. There was enough land allotted for the estate to expand to a half million, when the need arose. That need did not materialize, because the Garden was abandoned. But much of interest occurred before that fateful event.

When it came time to wean her children, around twelve months, Eve gathered nuts and fruits from plants that Van and Amadon had cultivated decades before. Knowing about the nutritional value of these foods, she made a potent liquid that well nurtured the little ones until teeth appeared.

Eve taught Lyla how to properly combine the Garden's produce to create nutritionally superior foods that would satisfy the needs of both the human and the Adamic type of body. Lyla then taught these things to her daughters and other mothers of the Garden.

There was no cooking done in the home of Eve and Adam. They ate only ripe fruit, nuts, and cereal grains. From the beginning they ate but once a day, around noon. Along with the foods produced in the Garden's fields, Adam and Eve regularly consumed the fruit and leaves of the Tree of Life growing in the center of the courtyard of the main temple.

The pair always dressed appropriate to the occasion. During the day, owing to the mild climate, they wore little clothing. When evening came, they donned wraps. Thus clothed it appeared as if light poured from their heads. There was no end to marveling about this fascinating phenomenon. Garden workers were endlessly intrigued by the faint violet glow emanating nightly from the bodies of their new world leaders. Most held that such radiance could only come from divine beings. To Adam and Eve it was simply the way of things. And after their appearance on Earth, supposed holy men and women were so depicted in art and stories, often including halos.

Indeed, they did seem to possess divine attributes. Adam and Eve had the ability to communicate telepathically over long distances. This is a function unique to the Adamic brain, an attunement to higher mind circuits that made telepathy possible. This ability was also present in their first offspring. But their access to the specialized circuit that facilitates telepathic exchange was suspended when their oath was broken.

One of their priorities during the first years was creating more and better schools. It had already been decided that the children of Eve and Adam would attend their own schools in the east of Eden until age sixteen. The Garden method of teaching was the divine method of experiential transference, wherein the older student teaches the younger. The young children attended classes just as the older, but their sessions were only half as long.

The children of the first Lyla and Lam grew right along with the Adamic family, though Lyla could not keep up with Eve in producing offspring; she bore only fourteen. She and Lam became well aware of the difference in temperament and ability between the offspring of their respective families.

The Adamic children were much more playful, risible, and creative; all were endowed with an excellent sense of humor and always was laughter heard when Adamite children were present. Play, humor, musical and spiritual appreciation are gifts bestowed by Adam and Eve. And, compared to humans, Adamic children were seldom hampered by fear or anxiety.

After age sixteen, graduates of the schools of the east transferred to the college in Eden's west, there to become student-instructors. While they taught the younger ones, they could also pursue advanced education in either horticulture or Garden administration, or as spiritual guides. These specialized classes were led by graduates of both schools.

The morning's instruction in the western schools, for non-specialized education, was gardening and agriculture. The afternoons were devoted to physical activity, games involving competitive play. The evenings were spent socializing, in developing friendship and learning the delicate skills that foster beneficial associations between persons, families, and social groups. But it was always the domain of the parents to instruct the children in matters pertaining to sex relations and religion.

There were seven categories of instruction in the western schools:

- Care and maintenance of the body
- Ethical behavior
- Group rights versus individual rights
- Earth history
- Trade and business relations
- Balancing emotion and duty
- Play, humor, and competitive games

With regard to personal behaviour, there were seven general laws that governed all Eden. The rules were adapted from earlier laws set down by the Prince and his staff, before they rebelled. The rules regulated several arenas of social activity and inner attitude:

- Sanitation and heath
- Social interaction
- Ethics of trade, inside and outside the Garden
- Fairness
- Home life
- Community relations
- Morality

Eve and Adam established two periods of worship each day. At noon all Eden's residents retired from their duties for a period of intimacy with their Maker. This public worship session was complemented by a period of private family worship in the evenings.

The Adamic family taught that prayer should come from the soul, and that petitioners should refrain from rote praying. Adam tried to convince Garden residents that, to be effective, prayer should be individualized and personal. And that they should pray not for things but rather for values. But he made little progress. Old, familiar ways often work against new and untried ways, even when the new is better.

The pair labored hard and long to provide a perfect example, but it was almost impossible to lead those who were ignorant, doubting, and fearful. However, some workers and guests did comprehend and whole-heartedly embrace the Adamic message and mission. Even though these supporters knew it would require many centuries, they faithfully looked to the day when their descendants would be allowed to join with those of Adam and Eve to create a grand new family, one possessing the best physical, intellectual, and spiritual traits of the combined violet and human races.

Wherever they were, Adam and Eve always demonstrated gender equality. This divine ideal was inherent and ingrained in Eden's children. Everyone took note of Eve's standing as Adam's equal. Deference to, and inclusion of women became part of nearly every aspect of Garden life, and that mightily impressed guests, laborers, and administrators. But chivalry was not abandoned; the tender feelings between male and female were always respected and fostered by both Eve and Adam.

Before they wed, the young adult children of Garden residents were required to complete a two-year course in preparation for the joys and demands of family life. At age twenty they were permitted to marry.

After being wed, Adamic couples would begin immediately creating families, unless they opted for some special assignment requiring training in a certain field of expertise. Those fields centered on family rearing, Garden administration, and trade relations, or on improving agriculture—crossbreeding and cultivation.

The Garden's policy regarding visitors was liberal under certain conditions. The applicants for entry must be:

- Unarmed

- Adopted (sponsored by a qualified Garden administrator)

- Aware of the purpose and plan of the Adamic mission

- Loyal to God and a supporter of the Adamic mission

If guests met these conditions, they would be allowed a short sojourn in the Garden. It was not unusual for guests to apply for school and residency once they beheld the inspiring grandeur, the bounteous beauty, and the soul-satisfying splendor of Edenic culture.

Chapter 18

FIRST HUNDRED YEARS

All went fairly well within the Garden for nearly six generations, though difficulties did frequently surface. Some Garden workers were inclined to believe the lingering doctrine of unlimited freewill that was associated with the Lucifer Rebellion 162,000 years before—its insidious lies finding easy and lasting reception in uneducated and prejudiced minds. The Nodites were especially displeased. They always protested the history of the Earth taught to the Garden's children, as it tainted them with the stigma of rebels.

Van and Amadon taught that the Nodite race was descended from Nod, one of ten administrators on the superhuman staff of the rebellious Planetary Prince. Van and Adam found that many of Nod's descendants were able administrators and loyal leaders. Their services were valuable in both Gardens, notwithstanding their protests against being labelled children of rebels.

These on-going disagreements created much trouble for Adam and Eve, in spite of many and diverse efforts to negate their influence on the more easily misled workers. Adam and Eve thought it better to have protesters and covert rebels in the Garden for education and assimilation. And some of them did cease their agitations when they beheld the earnestness and felt the sincere love of Eve and Adam. That proved more valuable and desirable than unrestrained freedom and wanton liberty.

But when Adam attempted to take Garden culture and divine ideals outside, he encountered fierce resistance. The world may have been ready for a biological upgrade, but it was still primitive socially, politically, and spiritually. Adam was forced time after time to scale back his plans and modify his approach to accommodate opposing forces that so stubbornly prevailed outside the Garden walls.

During their first one hundred years Adam often expressed his gnawing frustration to Eve, at one point saying, "Our plans are being thwarted not only by our enemies, but also by our unwitting friends and appointees in the villages. What can we do, Eve? Our original plan for world improvement is hardly progressing. Even our well-thought-out gradual adjustments and measured adaptations are meeting insurmountable obstacles, endless resistance, stubborn ignorance, innate hostility, even violence against our outposts."

As the century wore on, and with Adam always away on some emergency, Eve's great heart longed to see some sign of success, so that Adam might be encouraged, that he might see sure and certain progress was being made on more than one front.

Most of all, she longed for him to be home with her, raising their rapidly expanding brood. He worked harder than anyone in the Garden, never could either of them be called lazy or ease-seekers. Eve only wished to have him near. One problem after another kept them separated. She thought when their sons and daughters came of age they might take on many of Adam's duties and responsibilities, and they did prove helpful. But troubles were always threatening to expand beyond their control, beyond their ability to correct, fix, or negotiate.

And too, they each headed a variety of committees and councils, all of which required periodic meetings and group conferences. Most times the couple would spend only one evening a week in each other's presence alone, the seventh day.

Except for a few hours' they might be permitted to enjoy together at home, they were living nearly separate lives.

Right along Eve was always with child, always suckling one or two. She could not stray far or long from their home, there she was needed to manage her and Adam's sixteen hundred children and grandchildren who were born during that first century. But Adam ranged the Garden, even staying overnight on the mainland on occasion, going about as he did, trying to establish the foundations for strong relations with the mainland peoples, in both trade and culture. This was necessary preparatory work for the day when Adam and Eve could begin sending their progeny to the far reaches of the Earth.

Eve kept busy to avoid loneliness. In the evenings, while Adam was away, she would gather listeners for "story-telling time." Eve was an excellent teller of tales, and could draw on her long, long past. But most story requests were for tales about the worlds the pair lived on before coming to Earth. Adam was a great storyteller as well, and both were teachers of truth. Eve intertwined her fascinating stories with eternal verities and rich details about what one might expect on the worlds beyond their home planet.

Hard as the first century was, the couple pressed on. But Adam's time at home was always short and very often curtailed by unavoidable demands for his attention. Eve continued to bear children at the rate of one or two a year, depending on single or twin births. She never ceased building up the home and caring for family. She and Lyla were great comfort to each other. But Lyla's body was mortal, and she died eighty-two years after Eve and Adam arrived on Earth, having long since ceased bearing children. The original Lam passed on two years before Lyla the first.

Lyla's daughters had been well trained to take over as personal aides. In every way possible they filled her role supporting Eve, Adam, and their rapidly growing family. Long did that service last, ending only when the last wave of the Adamic race vacated the second Garden, forced out by increasing floods. Lyla and Lam's sons were equally well trained to replace Lam in supporting the Lylas as personal aides and "Keepers of the Story."

Many other human friendships formed during Adam and Eve's first century on Earth. Often did they entertain and interact with leaders from the mainland villages. And these relationships deepened over the years as one difficulty after another was confronted and solved with intelligent teamwork planned and led by Adam.

Most of their solutions required coordination of human and superhuman assets, the intelligent management of men, midwayers, and angels. But all this kept Adam busy and away from home. Eve fought loneliness because she well knew Adam had to be present where the problems were, and to see that solutions were properly implemented. Cascading events kept him always occupied. When he had to be away on their day of rest, it was especially hard for Eve. "Could I not see and be with him *one* day a week?" she asked Lyla on more than one occasion.

Adam and Eve's children did take on administrative responsibilities just as soon as they proved themselves able. That usually came after a period of apprenticeship and testing inside the Garden, later with probationary forays outside.

The Adamic children were loyal to their parents and their mission. But their problems always seemed greater and more numerous than their ability to solve them. Their enemies saw to that. The children were kept as busy as Adam with new and demanding problems. And their greatest difficulty was yet to come, a misstep that will precipitate an epic catastrophe for humanity.

Chapter 19

EVE AND CANO

One frequent Garden guest, Serapatatia, became a close acquaintance of Adam and Eve. He was a highly effective Nodite leader of certain mainland tribes and had been successful in swinging several villages to Adam's cause. It was welcome news when good news was scarce. This capable, deep-thinking man understood and whole-heartedly supported Adam and Eve's mission.

So impressed with his leadership were they that Serapatatia was invited into their home on multiple occasions to discuss difficulties and possible solutions for the many-sided problems of their mission. He was made chairman of the tribal relations commission, which meant many more meetings with Adam and Eve. But, increasingly, the conferences were primarily between Eve and Serapatatia, Adam being away so often on urgent needs. He and Eve ardently shared, and often discussed a common wish: to help Adam achieve more and greater successes.

Every year it was harder to focus on the long view, to avoid thinking of convenient or quick shortcuts. For five years this topic of helping Adam, of achieving more success and hastening progress, was examined and reexamined by Eve and Serapatatia. On most occasions they debated solutions and remedies that fell within the prescribed bounds of Adamic missions, but they sometimes discussed other solutions.

Eventually their meetings became private, Eve not wanting to upset Adam with speculations and ideas that could violate their oath or exceed their mandate. But their talks always remained speculative. Lyla of that time knew about these meetings but not the details. Later, with the help of Eve, she made a record of how Eve and Serapatatia's last meeting unfolded.

It was during the couple's one-hundred-and-seventeenth year on Earth that Eve's misstep occurred. One beautiful evening, when the Garden was well into its blooming season, Serapatatia brought an extraordinary young man to their private meeting.

After introducing Cano, Serapatatia said, "I hoped you would be pleased to meet this man who has done so much to advance your mission in his village. He shares our wish for the success of your and Adam's mission. Since your arrival, he's acted with wisdom and enthusiasm in spreading good will on the mainland."

Cano was in his prime and indeed an exemplary physical specimen. To Eve's trained eye, he was the best of humanity from the mainland. She had heard of but never met him. She knew Cano was the chief of his village and like Serapatatia, a staunch supporter of the Adamic mission and an able leader. When certain rebellious villagers were advocating war and removal of the "invading aliens," he insisted it was much wiser and more advantageous if his people keep the peace. He persuaded his village elders that exchanging goods with the Garden, rather than hostilities, would redound to their prosperity, famously declaring that, "In war, only destruction, evil, and suffering win."

Cano was aware that Eve and Serapatatia had discussed a variety of potential solutions to leverage the meager successes of the ordained plan. Even forbidden solutions were sometimes broached. Eve felt she must do *something* to help Adam. More

121

and more often he expressed frustration over the slow pace of progress on almost every front. A hundred years had passed and the amalgamation with humanity was still thousands of years away. Again and again Adam confessed to Eve his failing efforts. He once said in near exasperation, "The original plan is insufficient for the size and number of our problems. The Earth may be ready for a biological uplift, but the foundation stones for fraternity and morality are all but absent. And languages are so diverse and incompatible as to confound the angels." This statement and others like it troubled Eve, causing her to lean into impatience and think about quick solutions.

More than once Eve felt progress was in reverse. They both knew enemies of the mission were living and working in the Garden, and on the mainland. Those facts preyed on Eve's mind as well. The midwayers informed Eve that their detractors often worked subversively, stirring resentment in individual Garden workers and certain mainland villages. There were repeated attempts to diminish even their modest gains. Fierce resistance and frustrating delays so often accompanied their endeavors, great and small.

Year after year of stubborn and unsolvable challenges exacted a heavy toll on the couple. Big problems were always followed by even greater ones. As the first century wore on even meager gains were gladly accepted and roundly welcomed. Gradually, however, discouragement set in, fortitude and enthusiasm waned, and the pair *nearly* lost their faith at one point. But when it came time to act, they did not falter. Quitting did not suit them.

Eve took on Adam's frustrations thereby compounding her own. In fact, the whole family shared their weariness and dissatisfaction. Their children longed for an end to Adam's thorny problems and Eve's growing loneliness. To their credit the Adamic children worked tirelessly for even small successes, for their parent's sake, if not the mission's.

More than a hundred years of missing their children and peers back on Jerusem fueled Eve's feelings of helplessness and heightened her longings for advice. She prayed for patience, but patience was the first casualty. Eve had an unfortunate tendency to forget that any problem, any difficulty, standing athwart the divine will is solvable, that eventually the way of the Heavenly Father wins all contests, that goodness and righteousness always prevail in the end.

The most often discussed solution to several of Eve and Adam's major difficulties was, in Serapatatia's mind at least, only a slight deviation from the original plan. On this occasion, with Cano listening intently, Serapatatia said to Eve in complete sincerity and with deep concern, "Many times have we discussed ways of accelerating Adam's progress and realizing more success. After talking these things over with Cano, he came to the same conclusion as you and me: Having an Adamic woman mate with a Nodite man, such as Cano, would produce a perfect liaison for Eden and the mainland. After training, he would become a great leader bringing the world to Eden, and in time, taking Eden's culture out to the world."

This was pleasing to Eve's ears, especially now, having met Cano. She was impressed and intrigued by his bearing and proven leadership qualities, even more by his physique. As a highly skilled biologist Eve could recognize superior biology.

The schools of Eden taught that heredity is the foundation of character, that character has measurable and desirable spiritual potential. Eve well-knew this and, at that fraught moment, asked herself, 'Is this beautiful young man the solution to Adam's manifold difficulties?' This Eve later confessed during a conversation with Lyla. Eve withheld nothing about the tragic affair after she regained perspective.

Cano joined Serapatatia in pressing Eve, moving in closer saying, "Such a child would surely have offspring loyal to our cause. And their children would, because of their nature, ensure faster progress inside and outside the Garden. They would become a line of strong leaders, ones who carry both human and Adamic heritage. Such leadership would fit perfectly with your original plan, as I understand it."

Eve protested faintly, "On regular worlds, the Adam and Eve do not personally mate with the sons or daughters of men. And I cannot ask one of my daughters to. When I collect the fruit from the Tree of Life, the Garden's angelic voice, Solonia, always reminds me not to combine good and evil."

"What is regular about this world?" Serapatatia asked pointedly. "Even your own schools teach that the Earth is isolated, kept from the others like a sick animal. And are we not all sons and daughters of God? I must remind you that we are talking about doing good, not evil. Good intentions cannot produce bad fruit. And the voice in the garden must not know how very good your and Adam's intentions are, or how big your problems are. The Garden's plan is simply not working."

Serapatatia plied Eve further, repeating and amplifying his and Cano's persuasions. "It will be many lifetimes before your children and my children can be permitted to mate, according to the original plan. Until that far-off day, we will languish for the lack of real leaders. You need them now if this century is to be better than the last. Cano's child will help attain what you and Adam so much desire, and have been unable to achieve by any meaningful measure.

"Forget not that such a child will have yet more children, a line of leaders who will support and achieve the Garden's goals. By the end of your second century on Earth, you will have hundreds more able leaders at your command. And I hasten to remind you, the Garden's mission is in danger of stalling, even failing."

"Only upon reflection did I realize this alternate plan had been maturing in my mind until that day, when I met Cano," Eve later told Lyla. "It seemed, at that moment, as though Cano was *the* answer to a long-held prayer."

Not long after the default, Eve and Adam confessed to Lyla everything that led up to it, so that the hard lessons wrought from their error would be remembered for all time. The pair wanted humanity to know how such a far-reaching failure could come about under the rule of divinely appointed global administrators. The truth is that they were neither born perfect nor did they rule in perfection.

Serapatatia and Cano continued putting forth their reasons for an immediate Adamic-human liaison. Eve hesitated; she needed to think. But she had been thinking about it for five years.

Then Serapatatia made bold and said plainly to Eve with great authority and conviction, "The time is right! And our intentions are good. Therefore we cannot do wrong." And he was not in any manner insincere when he said to Eve, "If you or one of your daughters combine their seed with Cano's and produce a great leader, it will be a great relief to Adam, and a tremendous stimulus to the progress of your mission... our mission!"

With so little apparent progress to report, and lately seeing so much discouragement and frustration in Adam, Eve was mightily swayed. The more she listened to Serapatatia and the strikingly handsome Cano, the more she was persuaded to act in that moment. Little by little the brilliance and logic of these two enthusiastic men, their forceful assertions and righteous emotions were combining to melt away what remained of her resistance.

Into the evening the discussion went on. Without wholly realizing it, Eve was becoming convinced beyond all doubt. Reason tried to assert itself, but in the rarefied atmosphere of this intense meeting her fondest wishes—to help Adam speed their mission and allow him to be home more often—finally caused her reason, as well as the admonitions from the Melchizedeks, and the Voice of the Garden, to be set aside. So convinced were they of the efficacy of this scheme that it didn't take much more to tip the balance of Eve's resistance, to do the unthinkable, to go astray of the divine plan.

Serapatatia did not hesitate to use promises and flattery. He pointed out again, "Since our intentions are good and you are a direct descendant of God, we cannot fail. It will take centuries for the original plan to show results. Our plan would create untold advantages, even during my lifetime. Behold, Cano! Have you, in all your years on Earth, seen a finer man in the whole land?!"

And once more Serapatatia reminded Eve of Adam's meager accomplishments during more than a century, save for her and Adam's personal progeny, which at that time, numbered only sixty-three. Having mated those sixty-three and set them about procreation, the Adamic household had at that time 1,647 members, only a fraction of the half-million pure-line descendants the mission specified before mating with humanity. Their first century on Earth had indeed been difficult. So little had gone according to their plans and hopes.

And the second century wasn't beginning any better.

And now, here was this easy solution that had the potential to solve most of Adam's problems, or at least give him more time for rest and parenting their ever-growing family. Did her children not need their father?

Serapatatia and Cano wanted—all but demanded—that she regard their plan as an infallible panacea for Adam's most vexing and intractable challenges. Cano simply could not believe their plan was flawed, or that such powerful feelings could be misleading. And were not their intentions good, even the best?

Adam, as usual, was busy elsewhere, ever beset with manifold woes. At that moment he was attempting to arbitrate a dispute between troublemakers working in Eden's south and loyalist administrators from the north. Some of the protestors were advocating short-sighted changes in Adam and Eve's plan. Some were even calling for Adam's resignation as ruler of the Garden. It was taking all of Adam's attention; he was completely unaware of this fateful meeting of his mate, Serapatatia, and Cano.

Eve looked the man in the eye, knowing she was fertile, and feeling intensely the call to procreate. Cano watched her face, then moved closer. She saw he was willing and able. Suddenly they embraced and garments were pulled aside. All too quickly the eager young man and the beguiled Eve had consummated the act.

But Eve's mind reeled; she felt a disruption, a tearing away from spirit. She realized, though too late, this was a mistake. Seeing that Eve was immediately distraught, Cano and Serapatatia assured her, "We cannot be wrong, you will see."

Cano told her, with Serapatatia nodding agreement, "If you bear my child, I will raise him or her as you and Adam wish." They each took one of Eve's hands and kissed them, then departed. She sat there alone, dazed and deep in thought.

In an instant, the planet's celestial workers realized the gravity of Eve's disobedience. Adam sensed trouble and mentally called out, "Where are you? What has happened?" No reply. It was as if Eve was hurt or absent, Adam later reported to Lyla.

He was deeply alarmed and quickly summoned a midwayer to transport him to Eve's location. On finding her, the whole story spilled out. Adam fell to the ground, listening in shock, anguish, and disbelief.

It then became the duty of Solonia, the "Voice of the Garden," to censure them, to declare that Eve had violated the covenant with the Melchizedek overseers not to mate with humans until their family reached the specified number.

Solonia further reprimanded Eve: "Even before coming to Earth, it was my responsibility to warn you of the dangers of this assignment. And each time you partook of the fruit of the Tree of Life you were admonished not to mingle good with evil. Yet, today, you did. For all your training, and after the many warnings, the covenant has been broken, and the consequences are upon you, Adam, and this world."

"What will happen to my beloved?" asked Adam.

Solonia replied solemnly, "It is all but certain that she has already been reduced in status to that of Earthly mortal. And already has she lost the ability to communicate from afar, because of the severed connection to that which confers immortality and other powers you once shared. Her body will eventually perish, but you will live on to complete the original mission."

This filled Adam with an unbearable sadness, for he loved Eve with a superhuman affection. For a moment he pitied her, then imagined seeing her die. The thought of carrying on without her for tens of thousands of years was unacceptable. It was too much. He looked at Solonia, then at Eve, and an idea entered his mind. There was a way to equalize the error, another easy solution. He turned to walk away.

Instantly Eve realized his intent and cried out, "No, Adam!"

"My dear beautiful Eve, you shall not be mortal alone." She followed him, knowing he was about to repeat her mistake and thus reduce himself to her status.

Adam turned to her, his heart heavy as stone, "Remain with Solonia." She collapsed in tears as he slowly and determinedly walked away. Solonia came to Eve's side, attempting to comfort and console this now sorrowful and guilt-ridden daughter of God.

Adam soon found the object of his intent, a granddaughter of the brilliant Nodite woman who, a century before, had welcomed the pair to the western college. Laotta had taken her grandmother's name and followed her as dean of the college; she was visiting the Adamic estate that day. Adam had seen her land at the stable earlier, just as he was leaving for the day's work. Laotta was there to meet with the head of the eastern school, to coordinate the curricula of east and west. Oftentimes she, her mother, and grandmother, had worked on education committees with both Eve and Adam.

As Adam approached this comely creature she noted a strange look on his face. In a few words, he explained that he wished to mate with her, in order that he might share Eve's fate and become as she now is, a mortal.

There was hardly a woman anywhere who would not have wished to join with the magnificent Adam in procreation, under any circumstances. Likewise, every man would quickly accept an offer to mate with Eve. Cano felt himself the most fortunate person on the Earth at that unique moment. He had intercourse with a god, and she would likely deliver him a divinely endowed child.

Laotta knew of the plan not to mate with mortals. Adam told her that the original plan had failed and now needed adjustment. And during those times, multiple mating was common. Right away, Laotta agreed, and Adam's fate became the same as Eve's.

But Adam was terribly disappointed by Eve's transgression, to the point of grief and anguish. "How could she, after our long training, and after so many warnings not to do this very thing, ignore it all and mate with Cano, and in secret? Why did she not discuss all this with me? Did I lead her to this by my constant discouragements and complaints?" He wasn't angry; he loved Eve too much. At that moment all he could feel for Eve was sympathy. He pitied her as only genuine love can.

After mating with Laotta, Adam left. Eve knew not where. For thirty days he was absent, gone, out of touch. During this awful and dark time Eve fell into a hellish spiral of self-recrimination and lonely anguish. Clouds of guilt gathered and remained in her distraught mind. The pain of disloyalty rained down and the agony of failure flooded her being. Was Adam taken away for her error? Had he taken his own life? In her tormented state, the worst scenarios took root and repeated endlessly.

During those thirty days of Adam's absence Eve was inconsolable, ever reiterating the same questions and pleas, "What have I done? How could I have done this? Where is Adam? Father God, please bring him back alive and safe." She begged Solonia, and everyone else, "to find him before something dreadful happens."

But Adam didn't wish to be found. He took flight to the foothills of the coastal mountains in the west, roaming aimlessly, sorting out feelings and the now inevitable consequences of his intentional error. Meanwhile their children were suffering. It was difficult seeing their beloved mother in such distress and not being able to do anything to relieve it. They tried to comfort their stricken mother during their father's absence. Some feared Adam might not return, no one knew. Each day without him, not knowing his physical or emotional state, was all but unendurable for poor Eve.

Finally, Adam's reason, balance, and wisdom gained the upper hand and he returned to Eve and his disconsolate family. On seeing her beloved, alive and healthy, Eve was beside herself with tears of mixed joy and sorrow. Adam felt her emotional fatigue and exasperation. Now those feelings could begin to be replaced with hope. He took her in his arms and they wept. The children surrounded their wounded parents, also shedding tears. Solonia looked on in bereavement, for she knew that, not only had the Adamic family been severely traumatized, their magnificent Garden home was almost surely doomed.

When Adam finally returned, after this terrible time of crushing uncertainty and self-blame, Eve rejoiced like never before or never after. Her gratitude on seeing Adam's face, his forgiving face, was immeasurable. But she and her children were emotionally scarred by this affair. Their trauma was never fully forgotten, though forgiveness of both parents was gladly and freely given by all of Adam and Eve's offspring.

Right after Adam went away in defeat and retreat, the Garden residents heard the story of Eve's mating, and immediately blamed Cano. They whipped themselves into a fanatical fervor over the matter. Without Adam's leadership to cool their anger or contain their resentment, war was declared on Cano's village. The enraged Garden workers marched to the mainland and took the life of every man, woman, and child, and burned the village to charcoal.

Cano, the father of Cain yet-to-be, was killed in the raid. But Serapatatia was still wandering the Garden, lamenting his part in all this, suffering unbearable fear and all-consuming regret. He wanted to see Eve, but realized that would only create more trouble. The day after Eve and Cano's liaison, saddened and guilty, Serapatatia perished. Upon realizing what his ill-conceived plan had wrought—hearing the Garden workers blame Cano and knowing they would shed blood in retribution—this man of good intentions fell into a hopeless depression. He went to the river, filled his garments with stones, waded in, and threw himself into its depth.

Soon after Eve and Adam erred, it was Solonia's duty to recall the Melchizedek Receivers. She predicted the Receivers would confirm her opinion, that the pair would be reduced to mortal status. That they would die when their bodies wore out, and then be resurrected on a mansion world, as would an ascending mortal. They knew however, their lives on Earth would likely be several times that of an average human. All awaited the judgment from on high to know for certain Adam and Eve's disposition and fate.

Chapter 20

REPERCUSSIONS

On the day Adam returned Solonia spoke with the pair. She informed Adam of all that had transpired during his absence, saying, "After hearing of Eve's liaison with Cano, angry Garden workers betook themselves in madness to Cano's village, destroying it and everyone within. Cano was one of the first slain." A tear fell from Adam's eye.

"And Serapatatia?"

"Perished, by his own hand," replied Solonia. "But there is more troubling news: The villages and tribes loyal to Serapatatia are gathering forces to march on Eden, to avenge his and Cano's demise, with which they charge you. They will not hear that Serapatatia killed himself; they cast all blame on you and Eve. His family and allies living to the north are even now gathering an army to march on Eden."

Adam looked at Eve, then Solonia, and asked, "What are we to do now? What can we do? We did not come to Earth to fight or kill, even though many unnecessary deaths have already occurred, and more will likely follow our mistake. And I have not forgotten we have two children in the wombs of Eve and Laotta, one from each camp, both of which now loathes us."

Solonia spoke softly, saying, "If you are unwilling to defend the Garden, you must leave, or be killed yourselves. The midwayers have watched Serapatatia's avenging army grow. Its size and ferocity are well beyond what would be required to invade Eden and destroy all of you. They will soon be at Eden's gates. Others plan to attack by boat."

No sooner than she said that, Adam looked up to see the Melchizedek councillors approaching, all twelve. By their presence Adam knew without the least doubt that he and Eve had failed. And the immediate consequence of this failure would surely be their reduction to mortality status. He was right.

Adam pleaded with the council, seeking their advice. It was a sorrowful scene, but the Melchizedeks refused to advise him, saying it would violate their mandate not to interfere. They did offer co-operation, as much as possible, within the limitations of their authority. But they could not offer advice about what actions to take, per the instructions of their superior, the Father Melchizedek.

He turned and looked at Eve and Solonia, saying, "I have no taste, no training, and no desire for war."

Eve, still heavy with remorse and self-blame, asked, "Wither shall we go, Adam? The children and I need assurance and direction."

"We shall leave," said Adam with profound sadness.

"Where?" asked Adamson.

"We cannot go north," said Adam. "A hostile army is approaching from that direction. And we know there are warring and unfriendly tribes south of here. We have no ships to go west, over the sea. That leaves only the east, and the distant land between the great rivers."

Lyla and Lam were seeing and hearing all that went on. Adam called to them and said, "Send out the message, go to all the leaders and administrators. Announce a meeting for this evening. Convey the urgency, but assure them of survival, that we have a way, and we have the co-operation of the Melchizedeks. In spite of these grave setbacks, our Father's mission—even if compromised—cannot be abandoned, and I will not go to war."

Lyla hastened to the Father's Temple by fandor where scores of the Garden's supervisors were gathered in near panic over the imminent invasion. On hearing Lyla's message from Adam, they immediately sent out their lieutenants with the dire message, who in turn gave it to their subordinates, families, and friends.

Lam went to the aviary to send the message to every station, that all leaders should hasten to the Father's Temple to hear Adam and Eve address the emergency that very evening. Soon, the whole Garden community had heard of Adam's return and call to meet.

Before Adam's return the Garden citizens knew that an army was marching to destroy Eden and kill them for slaying Cano and Serapatatia. Some had thought Adam was dead, and Eve could not be expected to lead a war. There was much contentious debate as to what they should do. Despite widespread anger and disillusionment, even mistrust of their once infallible leaders, the crisis demanded strong leadership and it came as a great relief to know Adam was alive and calling for a meeting.

Twelve hundred men and women, including all the Garden's leaders and administrators, attended this gathering. They were weary from weeks of chaos and sorely in need of reassurance, for some workable plan of survival. Having no solutions of their own, all were relieved that their leaders were again in charge, that there was hope. The Garden workers were now willing to support their beloved, if not perfect, leaders.

While most of the children and elders remained at home awaiting a report about the meeting, Adam and Eve stood before those who did attend. Never had they seen such serious expressions on Adam and Eve's faces.

There was no cheering or adulation; it was indeed a tense and solemn occasion. "We come before you, our loyal leaders and faithful administrators," said Adam, "to admit the truth, that we, your assigned rulers, have made a great mistake. There will be a time and place to examine what happened and draw whatever wisdom we can to guide such decisions in the future. But now we must act quickly to avoid a deadly and pressing threat.

"I called you together this evening to tell you it is our plan to leave this Garden and create another. Eve and I have no appetite for war, nor would we have any of you die for our errors. Therefore, we must leave the Garden *now*. Return to your homes and collect the things needed for a long journey, for we shall depart eastward, to a new Garden site. We must leave tomorrow, by midday."

A confused rumble came from Adam's hearers. Some thought to object—this was the only home most knew. Many felt leaving would make them more vulnerable, and that the Garden was worth fighting for. But they hesitated to express opposition, for most dreaded the idea of war and knew they would suffer and die in such a conflict; all had heard the reports of the coming hordes. They wanted to know what new site Adam had in mind. "Where will we go? Will we be safe?" they asked. He raised a hand to quiet them.

"Before we came, when the Planetary Inspector's report was issued, the Garden's present location was deemed the best of three sites. One of the other two sites is to the east. And east is also the direction holding the least danger. Therefore, gather your families, assemble your supplies, collect your seeds, and choose the best of your herds. We shall travel to a land between two great rivers, there to begin anew, there to start a second Garden."

Two days after leaving, the midwayers brought reports of the Garden siege. Adam and Eve were informed that a great wave of avenging Nodites stormed through the gates of Eden. Others landed by boat along the northern coast and crossed the hills into the valley. The invaders found only small groups of mainland villagers pillaging the settlements, capturing animals, and squabbling over foodstuffs. The leaders of the army were bitterly surprised to find the peninsula was completely abandoned by Adam's family, the workers, and most of their animals. They did find the Tree of Life, joyously thinking it would bring them life eternal.

Later midwayer updates revealed that instead of pursuing Adam and Eve, the invading army claimed the territory, made camp in the Father's Temple and set a guard around the legendary tree. The leaders ate the tree's fruits and leaves each day, believing it was a source of eternal youth. After several years, and after the death of one who had been regularly consuming the tree's fruit, it was destroyed in a fire.

Looking back on their error, Adam and Eve realized they would have someday gotten all they wanted if not for impatience. This realization was perhaps the most agonizing and regrettable aspect of the failure of the first Garden—that and the suffering of their blameless children and loyal followers. It was impatience that made their children innocent victims of foresight abandoned, of faulty plans and disobedience embraced. "In my haste, I forgot," Eve said to Lyla, reflecting on the default, "that there are no shortcuts in the work of world building, no way around the divine way."

On another occasion, Lyla and Lam recorded Eve saying, "If I had not caused our mission to default, the entire world would have benefitted from the full infusion of our disease resistant violet blood. Such improvement is a primary part of Adamic missions, alongside intellectual uplift, and the enhancement of spiritual capacity. Most physical ills and moral degeneracy are eventually eliminated by the infusion of the violet strain. This is true on a normal world at least."

A related casualty of their default was the end of a fragile peace between the Nodites and the Adamites; long did the northern Nodites blame Adam and Eve for the massacre of Cano's village. That injustice ignited a perpetual enmity—wars that raged on for centuries between the aggrieved Nodites living north of the first Garden, and the Adamites living in the Euphrates valley. That legacy of vengeance always negated any forgiveness and good will that some of the wiser Nodite leaders attempted to foster.

There was yet another tragic consequence of the default, one that affects modern peoples. Adam reported that, although many grains and cereals were improved in the first Garden and carried with them to the second, many others were lost because of the hasty flight. Those seeds and strains were lost forever.

Chapter 21

JOURNEY TO THE SECOND GARDEN

Not long after leaving their beautiful, fruitful, and familiar home, Eve and Adam fell to the very bottom of regret and remorse, going apart and confessing to God such sincere repentance that the angels were moved to weep. It was at that moment the Spirit of the Father came to dwell in them, to assure them of continuing life, forgiveness, and his abiding love.

Adam told Lyla this fragment of God would indwell he and Eve all their days, to guide them even after leaving the Earth—and that someday all humans would receive this same gift of eternal indwelling. Never again did they doubt or question eternal survival, or God's forgiveness; and the challenges ahead tested them in every way.

On this journey the midwayers were indispensable scouts, advising Adam, helping the caravan avoid natural perils and hostile attacks. It was difficult at best, living in tents and under the frequent Mesopotamian rains. Day after day, month on month, men, women, and children pressed on with herd animals in tow. Occasionally, when the midwayers presented Adam with more than one option, he and Adamson would take a fandor flight for an overview.

Eve and Laotta were excellent company for each other as the caravan travelled. They led the women in forming a network for communicating movements, transmitting personal messages across their span, and relaying general news. Problems kept them busy day and night, all of them. The women also provided medical and maternal care as needed.

Adam was ever involved with routing details, movement timing, and other duties thrust upon him by this odyssey of thousands of exiled Garden workers travelling to an unknown land. Each day was exhausting, but they never again thought of shortcuts.

The living Lylas and Lams of that time did all they could to nourish and care for the pair, preparing their meals and beds, massaging Eve's great frame at day's end, heavier each day with Cain-to-be.

On the third day out from their ill-fated Garden, the caravan was stopped by a host of transport angels. They carried the official verdict on the pair's misstep. As expected, they both were reduced to mortal status. Still, it was a mighty relief to hear this:

"You are not adjudged to be in contempt of universe government. Therefore will you be permitted to resurrect with the mortals of the realm in conformity with dispensational and special resurrection policy currently in force. Eve's act was deemed a misjudgment in administration, not an intentional or antagonistic circumvention of divine rule. Adam's act demonstrated such loyalty to Eve as to offset his error."

This now disgraced pair who represent the last and lowest link in the living chain of divine ministers that extends from the Father on Paradise on down to Earth, would live and die as mortals of the realm. Though their lives would likely be many times longer, they would still have to enter the next life through the portal of death and await resurrection like any other mortal of flesh and bone.

In shock and sorrow Eve clasped her hand to her breast when she heard the next words from the official messenger attached to the angelic convoy:

"The Most Highs deem it wise to offer sanctuary on Edentia to all the material son and daughter's children. All over age twenty are to receive this offer. All under twenty shall be transported to Edentia."

It was grievous duty telling their children under twenty this news. All did not agree with removal; others were relieved. When the number of adult children choosing to leave for Edentia was tallied, Adam and Eve were crushed. But they did not in any manner reprove or reproach those who opted to forsake this dark and sinful world.

Almost two thirds of the adults chose Edentia. Not given a choice, every child under twenty was enseraphimed and readied for transport to the sphere of the Most Highs. When all were counted—the adults who opted to leave and children under twenty who were given no option—it totaled three-quarters of Eve and Adam's Earth family.

The pair was present to see their children off, to bid them a heart-wrenching farewell. And Adam assured all, "We shall meet again in an instant of time, relative to eternity." Still it was a tearful scene. Some of the under-age children were highly distraught about this forced exit, decrying it as unfair. But it was all to no avail.

When the last seraphim departed for Edentia bearing their precious cargo, the remaining children gathered around Eve and Adam in a huge mass, and all wept. Such sadness was never heard. This was the most devastating of all consequences suffered by these two erring parents and their now divided family. Lyla heard Adam utter these words of comfort to Eve, "They are out of the path of further harm."

With deeply furrowed brow Adam said to family and workers gathered around, "For we transgressors, the way is indeed difficult. But you have trusted us, and stayed with us, even after our failure. Now let us be on our way, to hasten that certain day of righteousness, when men and women of Earth live in harmony with God, and without such grievous consequence as to lose their children for a season."

The now reduced caravan, heavy with the sadness of a splintered Adamic family, and having the extra duties of those who were taken, again took up the journey. Adam and Eve, deeply disheartened, summoned their reserves of power and moved to the caravan's head, leading on in spite of losing so many of their Earthly brood. But, let this record show that the four hundred children who chose to stay on Earth with their mother Eve and father Adam, all led extraordinary lives that bore much fruit.

The midwayers kept Adam well informed regarding the army that took over the Edenic peninsula. He was relieved to know they were settling there, and not in pursuit. The Edenites had abandoned the first Garden none too soon, heading east and south on the ancient caravan trails.

Along the route, Eve and Adam took special precautions to ensure the seeds and spores they carried were kept safe. Fandors, dogs, goats, sheep, and certain other domesticated creatures, all inhabitants of the first Garden, were brought along to ensure a good start at the second. The caravan's destination was the land lying between the two great rivers, the Tigris and Euphrates, in the plains to the east of the first Eden.

When the residents of the region heard the king and high priest of the Garden of Eden was marching on them, they fled in haste to the eastern mountains. The weary travelers were relieved to know the prized locale had been vacated. They would not have to deal with resistance or hostility after their exhausting journey. It had taken nearly a year to complete the Adamic exodus.

Both Eve and Laotta delivered before the caravan arrived at its destination. Eve barely survived, even her strong heart was weakened giving birth to Cain. Laotta perished delivering her daughter, Sansa. Adam was present; he and Eve used their every skill but could not save the life of both Sansa and her mother. Once more their failure had spawned bitter consequences. A tear rolled from Adam's eye. Such were the added hardships of their transgression.

Eve took Sansa to her breast, along with Cain, the fruit of her transgression. Sansa was raised alongside Cain and, at an early age, proved herself able and wise. She matured into a woman of skill, talent, and charm, eventually leaving the second Eden to marry a chieftain living to the north, thereby improving relations between the Garden and the tribe of her new family. There, she introduced many ideas and ideals of violet culture.

It was a trying and tiring year travelling across Mesopotamia, camping in beast-infested jungles and ominous woodlands. When they did arrive, they encountered an unavoidable natural challenge. The Euphrates was at the peak of its annual flooding. The weary sojourners were forced to make camp west of the river.

It was six weeks before they could cross safely into the fertile land between the two great rivers. While they tarried, Adam and Adamson flew over the region to locate higher ground on which to start the new Garden. From these reconnaissance flights they began planning ways to control seasonal flooding, and to create reservoirs that would water the Garden during dry times.

After their default, Eve taught her hearers, Garden residents and guests, "Mercy is the way of heaven, even when the consequence of misjudgment is dire, even when innocents suffer. The family suffers right along with the wrongdoer. And my family has suffered much. You have seen the consequences of my error, the loss of the first Garden, the removal of so many of my Earth children, also our downfall to mortal level. And now, the world will lose Adam and me as well. But fear not, the Father will send more sons. Because of our mistake, we will eventually die. But the Earth will not be forgotten, it will not be abandoned. Always will you have the angels and midwayers to preserve civilization and advance spiritual progress."

Chapter 22

ESTABLISHING THE SECOND GARDEN

Reduction to mortal status meant forfeiting connection to the spiritual energies of the realm—those living energies that interacted so favorably with ingestion of the fruit of the Tree of Life to extend physical life indefinitely. It wasn't long until Adam and Eve noticed the first signs of aging. Their default ordeal, followed by the long and difficult journey, had taken a toll.

Their bodies were not nearly spent however. They maintained focus and nourished each other's hopes, thanks in great measure to becoming indwelt by the Spirit of the Father. They were fully determined and duty-bound to redeem what they could of this mission to the peoples of Earth in whatever time they had left. The inevitability of death and the certainty of resurrection on the mansion worlds was in their future. They estimated their now mortal bodies would endure for several hundred years, and that would allow them time to salvage some measure of the mission's original plan.

The peaceful occupation of their new home was a much-needed balm to the travelers. The evening after the caravan finally reached the chosen site, under a warm setting sun, Eve had her sons and daughters gather the entire company in order that she and Adam could say a few words of welcome and encouragement to the new occupants of the second Eden.

Lyla and Lam recorded Eve's words delivered to this gladsome group. All were feeling celebratory to be at journey's end, in a place where they could make a fresh start. It was certainly not as beautiful or developed as the first Garden, but it offered new hope and it was a safe place to raise their young. And there was fertile ground for growing good and abundant foods.

The pair stood atop a rock outcrop, where Eve said in graceful tones, "Family and friends, let us be about the Father's business to settle this raw but beautiful land. Security must come first. The rumors you have heard about wall-building are true. To the north where the two rivers come near each other, a wall will be constructed. It will have, like the first Garden, gates to control exit and entry.

"While some of us work on the wall, thus securing this land, others will begin plowing and planting ahead of next year's floods. Some seeds and shrubs must go in the ground now if we are to have enough to feed our children and animals next season. Eventually, when the supply outgrows our needs, we will begin trading foods and other goods, just as in the first Garden. Adam and I have more plans to share with you, when the time is right."

Adam then said with tremendous humility and sincerity, "Our greatest gifts on this Earth are your loyalty, devotion, and dedication. We thank you all, for every one of you was needed to give their utmost in our long journey. You did not hold back, and you did not lose trust in us. Those are gifts worth having and we cherish them.

"We shall, in one year's time, establish security, begin building a safe, permanent water system for drinking and irrigation, dig sanitation and disposal facilities, and begin to cultivate a variety of foods. This and more will be required if our mission is to continue and succeed. All this we will do while increasing our number, making more children, yours and ours.

"We will, in time, transform this new Garden into a world center of trade and learning. Between these rivers we shall grow our two families. We will raise many more daughters and sons to become strong leaders and wise parents. Creating excellent families is the essence of our mission. Civilization cannot survive without them.

"We cannot, however, neglect the Father, our loving, caring God who made the original plan for all the worlds. With your help the divine plan for the Earth will be salvaged, and a proper temple will be built.

"Tomorrow I will a select a team and put them in Adamson's charge. Their work will be constructing a temple for the worship of the Father of us all, in whom we exist, and He in us. This will be an ever-expanding temple wherein our children can receive spirit consecration and moral education.

"But these grounds must first be cleared, and a sanctuary raised. In this temple we may, every day, rejoice in the security of our Heavenly Father's love. And every seventh day, let that day continue to be one of rest, of friendly play, but primarily of prayer to, and worship of, our Creator Father."

"But tonight, we should rejoice, make music and dance!" declared Eve. "Now that we are here, we can celebrate safe arrival in a promising land. Too much suffering has been wrought from the past. But forgiveness has been received from on high, from my children, and from you loyal volunteers. Let us all celebrate this new beginning tonight and let us not languish or stumble tomorrow. We have all suffered much, yet our love and devotion to service endure. And while we rejoice, forget not our Father who makes all things possible, even new beginnings."

Everyone took that as a signal to unpack the instruments. Gathered around a bonfire the Edenites made wonderful music that night. Immediately the melodies prompted nearly everyone to dance. The harmony of sound and the release of laughter filled the night air as accumulated emotions found suitable expression in joyous celebration of their arrival at this final destination. Some music had been played almost every night during the journey, but such joyful merry making had not been seen or heard since leaving the first Garden. Now with sweet and fully earned abandon, they celebrated far into the night, singing and dancing beneath the stars and moon that shined so brightly over this, the second Garden of Eden on Earth.

Eve and Adam took pleasure in their children and followers' enjoyment. It was a welcome relief from the sadness that followed their default. The Adamic children took great comfort in their parents' obvious pleasure, the cloud of remorse and regret finally lifted from their heads, in a measure at least. Smiles appeared on the faces of Eve and Adam as they danced for the first time in over a year. Baby Cain and little Sansa watched in fascination, perched on their elder sisters' swaying hips.

The next morning work began for all. Many gathered materials for fires and temporary shelters. Others cleared brush and marked out home sites. Adam and Eve worked harder than anyone. To that fact, all would attest. By day's end everyone had secure and dry night shelters. A small group led by Adamson began clearing an area for the Father's Temple and laid the first foundation stone.

Some thought Adam and Eve were indefatigable, but Lam and Lyla knew better. When the day was done Lyla and her family attended to the exhausted pair, and then prepared their bed for a few hours of precious rest.

Every seventh day the Edenites enjoyed a welcome respite from the pressures and needs of rough living by communing with family and friends on the temple grounds. The Adamic family members had delightful senses of humor and play, and this helped keep spirits up the other six days of the week. Laughter that was largely absent since the default returned to these remarkable and resilient people. Everyone, Adamite and human, was positively affected by this innate attitude of cheerfulness and joviality.

Humor was essential to their health and well-being. By any measure, life in the second Garden was no bed of ease. The first Garden was luxurious compared to the undeveloped condition of the second, without roads, irrigation canals, or producing land. The legacy of Van and Amadon's eighty years creating and preparing the first Garden, and the improvements made during their first hundred years, were fondly recalled and sorely missed.

But Adam and Eve courageously led the way every day. They never avoided demanding or demeaning work. The sweat that appeared daily on their brow inspired all. No honest observer could ever say, "The workers toil while Eve and Adam play."

Chapter 23

CAIN AND ABEL

The first child born to Eve, almost two years after coming to the second Garden, was Abel. He and Cain grew up together. Even before they reached puberty, Cain decided to become a gardener, while Abel chose the life of a herder. These choices proved ominous and adversarial; young and arrogant Abel never tired of denigrating Cain, never let his half-brother forget that he was an inferior hybrid, even the evil fruit of their mother's disastrous decision. Choosing opposing occupations only compounded the brothers' alienation.

Traditional mores around blood sacrifice crept into both Garden cultures. Adam and Eve's detractors saw to that, sowing division over the matter wherever they could. Even the priests showed a marked preference for blood sacrifice. It was unfortunate that Adam and Eve had so little time to give religious instruction and set ritual practices in the second Garden. They were forced to delegate that role to the Garden's priests who they had trained in the first Garden. After their move to Mesopotamia, almost everything came down to compromise. There was a latent desire to return to the old way of animal sacrifice, and a persistent resistance to Adam's way.

Blood sacrifice was the only way some religionists wanted to pay homage to God. To his dismay, Adam was forced to give in to these traditions and practices of primitive religion, much more in the second Garden than the first.

Blood sacrifice or not, they needed laborers and administrators, not enemies. Eve and Adam well knew if they should forbid certain sacrificial rituals, some workers would leave and conspire to make war on the Garden. Back on the isolated peninsula of the first Garden, efforts to establish bloodless sacrifices had met with less resistance, but resistance none the less.

To make laws forbidding traditional sacrifices would only foment a rebellion in these spiritually ignorant but devoted Garden dwellers. They knew Adam's way, but many put their trust in the old ways, including Abel, who was strongly influenced by the misguided priests.

Still, Adam encouraged the offering of produce from the fields as temple sacrifices. But a sizeable number of the workers felt God and tradition demanded the killing of animals. Abel, having chosen the life of a herder, felt likewise, always and ever belittling Cain's bloodless, and therefore impotent, plant sacrifices.

And since the priests supported his view, despite Adam and Eve's often stated preferences to the contrary, Abel felt vindicated, empowered to flaunt his blood sacrifices and to belittle Cain's "paltry offerings." Cain seethed in resentment and suffered the pangs of social rejection. The brothers never ceased arguing and fighting over the merits of their respective vocations. And their parents could not reconcile the two.

As the sons grew so did their enmity. Abel would not let Cain forget that Adam was not his father, and that he was therefore inferior in status, intelligence, and ability. The two often fought physically, as Cain's anger was easily aroused. From boyhood on, Abel seized every chance to provoke his elder half-brother, until a well-nourished and irresolvable hatred grew between them.

One day during Cain's twentieth year—Abel's eighteenth—after more than a decade of the same accusations, aggravations, and physical altercations, Abel's words so infuriated Cain that he rose up and seized his younger brother's throat. Cain did not release his grip until he knew another accusatory word would not be uttered. Being the stronger, Cain overpowered Abel and he perished that day.

When his rage and anger began turning into the realization of murder, Cain fell into a chasm of dismay and guilt. He staggered away from the scene in disbelief as the dogs nudged Abel, yipping and fretting, knowing something was wrong. The dogs watched as Cain ran as fast as he could to the river's bank. There he sat until near sunset, dazed, staring at the swift waters, and thinking about what he had done, and what to do next.

Not long after he died, Abel's confused and leaderless dogs did the only thing they knew and drove the sheep to their nightly stable. When they arrived early without a shepherd, the household knew there was trouble. And when Eve was informed, she felt a terrible dread.

Cain's stormy mind finally settled on the irrevocable fact that he had indeed murdered his half-brother. The certainty of grim consequences bore down on him. He briefly thought about leaving without delay, taking a fandor to a distant land never to be seen again by his family. But instead, he slogged home, to the mother who loved him.

Adam was busy elsewhere, tamping down one of his never-ending problems. As Cain approached, Eve looked the young man in the eyes and knew that her worst fear had materialized. He blurted out his crime and dove into Eve's bosom. As they wept in sorrowful embrace, Eve hated once more what she had done to precipitate this angry killing of one of her children. And now, her error would leave an indelible scar on the heart of her and Cano's lonely, traumatized, bastard son.

To say Eve grieved over Abel's death, and the absence of her other children would be a profound understatement. Her grief seemed not to end. Each consequence followed close on the heels of the last. Eve endured so much emotional trauma — so many children removed from the Earth, and now an eighteen year-old son was killed by another son.

Eve never became impervious to feeling, never tried to numb or shut out the negative. Neither did she attempt to blame others, to put her burden on them. She bore this repeated emotional agony with grace and courage. This brave soul did not seek escape of any sort. Her courage and resolve revealed a being possessed by genuine wisdom and hard-won maturity. Eve's combined mortal and superhuman faith gave her the spiritual strength to face severe consequences, even the murderous death of one child by another.

Adam understood what she was going through, in a measure. They shared this self-inflicted burden. Sharing it afforded the strength and endurance needed to finish what they started, albeit far short of the original aim.

Before this, Cain had a low opinion of his parent's religious practices and beliefs, but now after many tears shed by both, when his Mother said, "My son, let's pray," he acquiesced. It was during this heart-felt petition that the Spirit of the Father came to indwell Cain, just as it had come to his parents on the second day out of the abandoned Garden. The answer to his prayer came as well. He was to leave Eden, for the good of all.

Cain immediately began gathering the things needed to leave his home forever. How he could, in one day, kill a sibling and then receive the Father's spirit indwelling, was so contrary to his immature logic and youthful understanding that he could no longer think. But he acted; he did what he must, while Eve did what she most disliked. She summoned Lyla and Lam to retrieve Abel's body. His was the first burial of a family member in either Garden, notwithstanding Laotta's unfortunate death. The whole family attended, except Cain, who had departed for "the Land of Nod," the morning after that strange and infamous day.

Among the Mesopotamian Nodites Cain became a renowned and respected peacemaker. And it was there he married. His wife, Ramona, gave birth to Enoch who grew to be a prominent leader of extraordinary achievement and a legendary man of God.

Cain did, in a way, make good on Cano and Serapatatia's prediction that he would become a leader. He and Remona deftly and skillfully brought the Nodites and Adamites together at the table of peace. Good relations between the eastern Nodites and the Adamites of the second Garden lasted for centuries, unlike relations with the estranged Nodites they left behind, Serapatatia and Cano's tribes living north of the first Garden.

Lyla and Lam of that generation very much loved the two young men, so Abel's death and Cain's absence caused them sorrow and consternation, which was only a small measure of what Eve and Adam felt about Abel's untimely death, yet another troubling reminder of their error. The night after Cain left, Lyla asked Eve about he and Abel. She wanted to know, "Why could they not make peace?"

Eve told her, "If Abel could have lived into a third decade, he likely would have become a different person. Both my sons were shadowed and haunted by our default, especially Cain. They grew up in less than favorable conditions in the aftermath of the loss of the first Garden.

"Surroundings strongly influence the child, but heritage takes over as years pass. Both possessed good physical, intellectual, and spiritual heritage. That overarching fact asserts itself eventually. Had Abel lived just ten years more, perhaps he and Cain would have made peace, eventually tiring of their boyhood rivalries. This is the first principle of child rearing: Heredity is the foundation of character, and character eventually overcomes environment. At least now, Cain's unique heritage can assert itself. I am sorry it could not happen here, but in the far-away Land of Nod.

"There is a difference between our children of the first Garden and Abel, the first born of the second. He grew up under difficult circumstances and developed habits of aggression. And since Cain knew all about his origin, he never felt like he belonged. After he took Abel's life, we prayed. He received assurance of forgiveness by reception of the Spirit of the Father. And he felt directed to leave Eden. As much as we disliked doing so, Adam and I encouraged him to go, because there might never come a time when he would not be a bitter reminder of our failure, and the irretrievable losses of the first Garden."

Chapter 24

LIFE IN THE SECOND GARDEN

Because the Garden workers brought superior seeds and a variety of hardy domesticated animals from the first Garden, they held many advantages over the native tribes residing beyond the two rivers that surrounded them.

It wasn't long after arriving that Adam and Eve began sending their children and administrators as ambassadors to the local settlements, seeking to establish friendship and trade relations. The pair fully understood that trade ties, where both parties are advantaged, are far greater than all the speeches, wishes, and dreams about peace. The last thing they needed now was more enemies and war. As they left their sweat in the unprepared soil, remembrance of the default plagued the Adamic family, especially those who had experienced the splendor and refinements of the first Garden. Work was so difficult and unending.

In some ways the laborers born and raised in the second Garden were better for not knowing of the beauty, grandeur, and abundance of the first. After Adam and Eve's deaths, the truth about it gradually grew into legend and later myth. Memories of the two Gardens of Eden became confused and conflated. Facts became fictions and were crystalized by the teachers and priests of later generations. Over time, historical legends and traditions became sacred scripture about a shadowy and evil beginning of life on Earth.

The father and mother of the violet peoples proved themselves worthy mortals in the second Garden. One night, Solonia said to them, "You have borne your lesser status with much grace, perseverance, and courage. You have faced every trouble without complaint or retreat. I believe the Melchizedek Receivers would approve of all you have accomplished in the second Garden, and how much more you will do, if you do not give up, or give in to impatience once more."

Adam was endlessly busy setting up schools, ambassadorships, and coordinating the training of laborers, administrators, and spiritual guides. Eve made certain that family was the focus of the Garden. Often, she and Adam would repeat this when imparting instructions: "As goes the family, so goes the community, the nation, and the world. The health of any society is directly related to the health of the family."

It was wise, and crucial for their mission, that Eve and Adam work unceasingly to create lasting institutions, religious and secular, within the Garden. And they worked diligently fostering good relationships outside, with the surrounding tribes.

Already was the pair planning for a time when they would not be on Earth to manage the family and culture they were creating. Otherwise, the whole Edenic project might fail, lose its uplifting influence on human culture by the attrition of time and the stultifying effects of primitive traditions. The wise policies and provisions they initiated and promoted, before their deaths, made for a relatively smooth transition when they ceased living on Earth.

Adam and Eve's first two sons of the original Garden became highly effective leaders. The first born, Adamson, established another center of Adamic culture north of the second Garden. Their second son, Eveson, was also an invaluable aid to his parents. And one of the sons of Eveson stepped up to lead the Adamites when his time came, after his parents' deaths.

Seth was born to Eve and Adam during the twelfth year in the second Garden. He showed a marked interest in spiritual affairs, which led to his appointment as head of the Garden's priesthood. Seth's son and grandson taught superior ways of group worship. They then took these advanced religious practices to the tribes surrounding the Garden, even beyond.

Eventually, a Sethite priesthood came into being and they officiated at ceremonies, marriages, and funerals. They were also teachers of health: physical, intellectual, and spiritual health. Some trained and served as physicians, others as advisors on matters of sanitation—primarily safe water and waste disposal.

Over the years, diet evolved among the violet race. Grains, fruits, and nuts were all the Adamic family consumed in the first Garden. After reduction to mortal status, on the caravan trip to the second, their diet expanded to include all plant foods. None of the first generation of the first Garden ever ate animal flesh. But meat was eaten in the second Garden— and early on—although Adam and Eve never ate animal flesh as a regular part of their meals.

While Adam and Eve lived, and long thereafter, the influence of Garden culture on neighboring tribes was profound. The Nodite remnants residing in the area were constantly inspired to higher personal, cultural, and social achievement by the Adamic example. In a limited sense, and by the stalwart dedication of their service, the violet peoples were fulfilling Eve and Adam's greatest desire: to see the Earth improving materially, socially, and spiritually. The ingenuity and quality of metalwork, pottery, and clothing that issued from the Garden deeply impressed the tribes living nearby. That and the religious teachings of Seth and other Adamic children created a wealth of trade and good will with local peoples.

Shortly after its establishment, the second Garden became the center and driver of a system of commerce that spanned Mesopotamia and the mountains to the east. It became widely known as a source of advanced literature, of fact-based learning, of superior art and high culture, the highest on the planet at that time, by far, according to midwayer reports.

The Adamites produced talented architects as well. All who entered the Garden were awed by the height and sturdy construction of the buildings, as well as their artistic adornment. They were amazed by the grandeur of the landscaping. Not uncommon was the Garden guest who, upon entering, felt he or she had been transported to a heavenly realm.

The schools taught gardening, horticulture, wood, metal, and textile crafts, and livestock hybridization. Some students went into advanced spiritual education and ethical training, hoping to qualify for the Sethite priesthood.

Never since has the world had such an excellent system of combined education by such an informed group of teachers of health, family life, industrial arts, and religion. As a result of the work of the Sethite evangels, Garden culture spread from villages around the Garden to north Africa, east to India, even to far eastern Asia, China and Japan. Eventually, Adamic culture returned to the region of the first Garden on the way to Europe. Over time, the spread and application of Sethite teachings made many thousands of lives better.

The violet race had a tremendous impact on every aspect of Earthly living. The infusion of Adamic genes and the establishment of superior culture, sooner or later, positively affected the majority of the world's inhabitants—in body, mind, and spirit. Often all three.

During and after their brief sojourn on Earth, mankind gained a new and better concept of God, and a truer picture of the magnificent cosmos in which we all live. Even though their mission defaulted, and the story about their lives became distorted and confused by faulty human beliefs, our world benefited immensely from their living presence, their actual work, and most significantly, from their hereditary contributions.

During Adam's final year, his 530th, the attending Lyla recorded this remark, "It would not be unthinkable, in epochs to come, for Eve and me to return to the Earth. Whether or not we return, we shall always keep this world in our prayers. It is the world where God came to indwell my mate and me. More descending sons will arrive to enlighten the children of the Earth after I leave. I know not when, only that they will come."

Chapter 25

FINAL ACTS

Eve and Adam alone produced forty-two children in the second Garden and sixty-three in the first. Many of the successes of the Adamic mission after the default were the result of the leadership and labors of these one-hundred-and-five pure line offspring, particularly their first-born, Adamson.

It is noteworthy that some success was also achieved by the significant contributions of Cain and Sansa.

Life as an Adamic child began with a well-balanced, diverse education. The Edenic schools offered courses to Adamites, Garden residents, and visitors, in architecture, economics, trade-relations, agriculture, sanitation, science, metallurgy, many other crafts and advanced skills useful to Earth's inhabitants of that day. But the heart of all their teaching was spiritual guidance.

The Adamites had, by far, the most innovative schools on Earth for religion and commerce. Besides learning varied skills and trades, students obtained instruction in music, humor, art, and the wise use of that ubiquitous youthful love of adventure.

Eve and Adam's family members always exemplified the soundest methods of child rearing. But so little of the Adamic teaching found its way into either sacred or profane history, becoming lost in religious myth making.

When the second garden became a stable and growing success, and when Eve and Adam began making plans for the continuation and expansion of Garden culture after their death, they settled on a project to gather the highest type of women from the surrounding tribes and impregnate them with the Adamic strain. Eve was made head of the committee that chose these women. She selected the future mothers largely from the Nodite tribes.

Of the 1,682 women who were impregnated with the Adamic life plasm, 1,570 of their children lived to adulthood. After impregnation the mothers returned to their tribes and villages to raise these hybrid children. This plan eventually inaugurated a global diaspora of violet heredity and culture that somewhat offset the default.

Eve and Adam's adult children who chose to remain on Earth, along with the violet children born in the second Garden, plus Cain, Sansa, and the 1,570 surrogate children who survived—they and their offspring eventually transformed a raw, savage culture into a global civilization that endures and progresses, even today.

After Adam and Eve died their progeny faced a formidable challenge in fulfilling the mission of spreading the Edenic culture to every corner of the world. To meet this challenge they did not resort to war and conquest. Instead they grew. And each time their numbers exceeded the land's capacity, they sent out a wave of well-trained Garden emissaries.

These violet-skinned emissaries went out in every direction and married into the better tribes—mostly Nodite in the beginning. Dissemination of Adamic lineage and culture caused civilization to flower again and again right up to the European renaissance. Adam and Eve always taught that a sustaining civilization of celestial grandeur and divine elegance would someday come about, no matter the setbacks, delays, and betrayals.

On one rare occasion, when the Lyla and Lam of that day were alone with the then aged Adam and Eve, Lyla asked, "What would the Earth have been like if the first Garden had not failed."

Eve told them, "The Life Carriers are responsible for designing biological formulas that will flourish in a given planet's ever-evolving environment. They are permitted to experiment with that life, but only on certain planets and within certain limits. This world was designated as one such planet. A unique experiment was attempted here, a plan to have the Prince's staff mate with the most advanced humans. That original plan called for eventual mating of those offspring with members of the later appearing Adamic family. Expectations were that a group of exceptional beings, great leaders and teachers, would come from these liaisons. But when the rebellion broke out, long before Adam and I came, that plan had to be abandoned.

"Following the arrival of a pair of our order, a normal world enjoys rapid progress in the primary concerns of mortal living: health, education, and spiritual character. The father Adam and mother Eve sent to evolutionary worlds live on for tens of thousands of years, their bodies being attuned to the energy currents of the cosmos and complemented by the life-sustaining nutrients of the fruit of the Tree of Life, culminating in endless youth, perpetual regeneration.

"Each Adam and Eve work to ensure that Edenic culture is eventually exported to every continent, every nation, even every family. All the while, the Temple in the Garden serves as a global center of worship where God's actual representatives may be greeted and learned from. The Father's Temples on normal worlds become places of spiritual pilgrimage for all the planet's inhabitants. You would marvel at the methods of education and the ways of training little ones on such worlds."

Then Adam added, "Normally, after the Adamic infusion, gains are made in every field, and one invention or discovery will lead to many others. And that eventually creates a society whose members have time for leisure. During such times of rest and retreat, original thinking and meaningful discourse develops the wisdom that permanently elevates humanity.

"Eventually the normal world will ring with truth, fill with beauty, and set a course for perfect goodness. Love abounds on such worlds as global peace and fraternity unites all into one family. At some point people cease dying, and instead, translate their souls directly to the mansion worlds, bypassing natural death entirely. In later days humans become advanced to a point that they may also bypass the mansion worlds, going straight to the sphere of the Most Highs, Edentia. You can scarcely imagine the advanced ages of Light and Life.

"On every world, when the Adamic culture reaches full fruition, the Heavenly Father sends other sons—divine teachers to further enlighten and spiritualize the world—until it attains the intended destiny of all inhabited worlds: age after age of increasing Light and Life. Those ages lead to other bestowals, but it is difficult to portray this ministry to minds that have little or no concept of cosmic evolution or divine destinies."

Eve offered this overview: "In spite of our stumble in the first Garden, important gains were made in the second. Adam and I love the people of this world and regret we will not be here to guide them into the ages of Light and Life. But I suspect we will not be far away. And we are leaving our children to complete our mission. Adam and I, because of our unique experience, could become advisers on the problems of establishing Gardens on other quarantined worlds. The hard lessons of our incarnation are valuable, and not just in our local universe. Even a poor example can be educational. And it is not unthinkable that we, or our children, could return here in some capacity.

"Only recently we received an intriguing message from the ruler of this universe, the Paradise Creator Son, Michael. He spoke of his impending mission to this world. Such an epochal revelation would be highly unusual and a supreme blessing to Earth."

And that veiled promise became a reality when Michael of Nebadon incarnated as Jesus of Nazareth.

In various and significant ways, the Adamic contributions have not been surpassed. The Mesopotamian culture became the source of a social fuel that powered and propelled civilization. Violet genes enrich every life with humor, play, compassion, love of adventure, and endless creativity. And even today, we eat foods that were improved by the pair.

While they still lived and worked in the second Garden, Adam and Eve created a system of education that included insiders and outsiders. Much was achieved in the realm of cultural exchange by simply offering free instruction in the advanced arts of metalworking, invention and manufacture, reading and writing, education and science. Students took this knowledge to their villages. And this practice continued long after Adam and Eve died.

All Garden visitors were disarmed upon entering, and they were required to have a sponsor. Prior to their visit, volunteer sponsors would go outside the Garden to meet with and instruct candidates for admittance. The volunteers ensured candidates were familiar with the idea and belief in one God, the Universal Father. Before being admitted, the ways, the laws, and the purpose of Garden life were explained. And before issuing a visitor permit the sponsor would obtain a sacred oath to uphold the tenets, customs, and rules of the Garden.

The laws of both Gardens prohibited killing. All residents and guests were taught that humans are potential temples of God and that it's wrong to destroy such a being for any reason other than self-protection and family survival.

Constant attention to creating and expanding trade was the greatest peacemaker in the Garden and beyond. The second Garden became a renowned world center of culture and trade, and it remained so for many millennia—until the weather patterns changed and desert claimed the Euphrates valley.

One of the greatest gains from Eve and Adam's brief tenure on Earth was the elevation of woman. Time after time, when he taught in the Garden's schools, Adam would say to his students, "Eve is not my inferior. The sexes are created to be co-equal, co-habitating parents of good families. The man and the woman both contribute to the making of a child. Have you not noted the traits of both the mother and the father often appear in their children?"

Before the deaths of Adam and Eve, they arranged for certain meritorious angels to remain on Earth in their stead, to promote brotherhood and help the Adamic descendants advance violet culture. Eve told Lyla that all angels chosen for this work were part of Solonia's group of ministering helpers whose special ability it is to foster global fraternity and improve inter-family relations.

Chapter 26

ADAM AND EVE'S DEATH

By human standards, the pair lived very long lives, well over five hundred years. The message from the Most Highs assured them that, after dying, they would join the stream of human survivors from Earth and sometime be resurrected in new bodily forms. They would be permitted to take up life where they left off, returning to, and reclaiming citizenship on Jerusem.

As death approached, they looked forward to being with their whole family, including the one hundred children they produced before coming to Earth. Near the end, Eve and Adam rejoiced in knowing they and their children would not only survive and reunite but would be permitted to join the endless parade of Paradise ascenders on the long pilgrimage to meet God, just as will every surviving mortal of Earthly origin.

Eve died first, at 511, of heart failure. Adam carried on nineteen years after Eve. Then he too succumbed to worn-out organs. The Lyla and Lam of that day attended the burial, a remembrance and celebration held at the center of the Father's Temple. The remains of the mother and father of the violet race were interned beneath the floor of the Garden's main temple, a tradition still practiced by certain religions.

In her eulogy, Lyla spoke these touching words about Adam and Eve, "They taught us our Father never ceases sending sons and daughters from the Paradise center of all things and beings. Some of these divine creators select a segment of space in which to set up their own 'local universes,' eventually comprising ten million inhabited worlds. They create many orders of beings, descending teachers and administrators who enlighten and advance each of the inhabited worlds. These sons and daughters come close to us because they love us. I know that Adam and Eve love the people of Earth, many of whom are their children and grandchildren. They told me they will always work for our advancement, even when they are physically absent. Our friends and mentors are gone, but the fruits of their labors will remain as long as our world endures."

Though they both erred, just once, they persevered and triumphed. After the departure of Van and Amadon, and after Adam and Eve died, no longer were there visible representatives of the government of God anywhere on Earth. And that was the situation until a Melchizedek was chosen to incarnate thirty-four thousand years later. Once again, a Son of God descended to Earth and advanced the light of truth.

Thirty-four millennia may have intervened between Adam and Melchizedek, but all that time the angels and the midwayers were working behind the curtain of invisibility, continuing to advance and promote Edenic culture. The story of Melchizedek's bestowal life must be told too, for it was founded in the Adamic bestowal. And Melchizedek paved the way for Earth's unique-in-a-universe bestowal, a Creator Son, Joshua ben Joseph of Galilee.

Because of the unceasing efforts of a host of beings working on Earth, the Adamic culture endured and bore much fruit, and does yet. Eve and Adam's bestowal prepared the way for two subsequent divine and epochal revelations. Their work laid a spiritual foundation for the world, one that Melchizedek would later build upon. Michael, in his role as Jesus, then sanctified and perfected the epochal teachings of both of his predecessors.

Because of Eve and Adam's life-long spiritual ministry and civilizing work, and that of their successors, a city of God now exists in the inner life of every normal-minded human, one that each person can visit within, where the Father's Spirit dwells.

The five-hundred-year mission of Adam and Eve left the Earth in far better condition than normal evolution would have. This is true despite retrograde losses and theological inertia — the inevitable lot of a world without superhuman leadership. But human physiology, intellect, and spiritual attunement were all improved, which quickened the pace of global civilization.

Well before Eve and Adam died, the ideas and ideals they taught were introduced, even embraced by many groups, and divine truths were lifted to unprecedented heights. A quality civilization is based in the best human thinking and acting. "Good people create a good civilization, not the reverse," taught Adam. "A worthy civilization cannot be created without a broad base of good people. Especially is this true of democratic peoples and nations."

Adams and Eves, though they have roots in God's perfection, are not born perfect. According to the Lyla of that time, Solonia, the angelic Voice of the Garden, while attempting to comfort Eve during the thirty days of Adam's absence, said this repeatedly, "Perfection is our eternal goal, not our origin. Our merciful Father of Heaven has already forgiven you."

When all costs and benefits are recited, Adam and Eve contributed much wealth to the Earth. Eve did falter; she succumbed to persuasive words about personal liberty, betrayed her authority, and disregarded her oaths. And her loving mate loyally followed in disobedience. But, after their error, she and Adam did not give up, go astray, or join the rebellion. They bore up to their responsibilities and never again stumbled in their duty to redeem and fulfill, to the best of their abilities, the remnant of the divine plan for their cherished evolutionary home.

In the second Garden Adam and Eve established a foundation for the most advanced culture the world had yet seen. The so-called bronze and iron ages took origin with them. An age of inventiveness and the drive toward greater social unity began with Adam and Eve, and it persists today.

Their improved alphabet sparked a revolution in literacy and communication. Nearly every other aspect of religious, social, and commercial life was in some manner improved by them. A new reverence for God and a richer understanding of our Universal Father may be their greatest achievement and finest legacy. They ever taught one God over all, and in all. That monotheism became the foundation of a progressing civilization, as later expanded and illuminated by Melchizedek and Jesus.

Chapter 27

VIOLET DIFFUSION

Their firstborn, Adamson, lived up to his father's prediction. He became an effective leader and helpful assistant to his parents in the work of securing and establishing the second Garden.

The Lyla of those days reported that Adamson left the second Garden and went north and east, up to the Caspian Sea region. There, on its southern shores, near the Kopet mountain range, he set up another center of violet people. For thousands of years—from the second Garden, and from Adamson's northern outpost—poured forth an unbroken stream of new vitality, high culture, and innovative thinking.

Adamic culture achieved many lofty goals through mechanical inventions and cultural enhancements born of expanded creativity, all conceived and nourished in enlightened spiritual worship practiced and taught by Adamites. Eve ever reminded her students that, "Worship is the fountainhead of creativity."

Adamson and his wife had thirty-two children before the first Garden was abandoned. But then she and all their children left with the seraphic transports for Jerusem that awful day on the caravan route. Later, well after the second Garden was established, he expressed a desire to travel, to go in search of Van and Amadon's highland home in the Himalayas. And it was there he met and married a Nodite of extraordinary lineage. Ratta was the last in a lengthy line of leaders who went back to the days before the rebellion. With this woman, Ratta, Adamson raised sixty-seven more children. Those sixty-seven became the founding population of the northern center of violet culture.

While he still lived, Adamson did not forget his parents. Every seven years he and Ratta would travel south for a visit with them and the rest of his family.

Following his parents' advice, and with the assistance of the angels and the midwayers, Adamson's second center of Adamic culture grew until it was well established as a renowned source of revealed truth, a wellspring of unprecedented innovation, and an oasis of enlightened living.

By 19,000 BC, the Adamite offspring had created a real nation of four-and-a-half million mixed race people. From the two Adamic centers there flowed a stream of violet traits and violet culture to neighboring tribes and well beyond, eventually spreading to India, China, Africa, Polynesia— everywhere but the Americas where the isolated red man struggled to form a lasting civilization, having missed the violet infusion.

Before Adam and Eve arrived, Van taught in the Garden's school that, "The original Melchizedek plan called for one million Adamic children to go to the Americas to join the red peoples to the violet." But the default of the first Garden effectively wrecked all such plans.

From Adamson and Ratta's progeny came a line of great leaders and administrators. For thousands of years their descendants kept the robust Adamic culture alive, ever so often sending their surplus numbers out into the world to mate with the better human types. These immigrants travelled in every direction, transporting with them new ideas, new ideals, and a higher culture.

Those progressive cultural seeds later took deep root in Greece, and in China, eventually flowering in both empires. Dormant seeds of Adamic heritage do still occasionally sprout and blossom; the giants of human achievement are most often expressions of the latent reserves of violet blood still flowing in mortal veins.

The original Lyla once asked Eve, before Adamson was born, "How long will yours and Adam's children live to be?"

Eve replied, "First generation Adamic offspring will likely live to four hundred years. Each generation thereafter will slowly tend toward the average human lifespan. And our children will eventually lose the abilities that Adam and I have; extended vision to see the midwayers, the Melchizedeks, and the angels who attend us all. Telepathy across distance, all of it will gradually vanish.

"Diminishing longevity is part of the Edenic plan wherein the Heavenly Father sends his children to fraternize with humanity, in the form Adams and Eves. Yes, it is inevitable that the Adamic children's lives will become shorter and shorter, but human lives will become longer as they are infused with the Adamic heritage. Adamic bestowals are in fact God meeting humanity in recognizable form, then raising humans to Godlike perfection. That is the final goal of human civilization—and each divinely indwelt individual who chances to pass through it."

The later appearing Lylas recorded that Eve's prediction about the longevity of her and Adam's offspring came true. Adamson, their firstborn, lived to the age of 396 years.

When the violet race marries into the human race, as did Adamson, the very heart of the Adamic bestowal plan is realized. Over the course of ages, the blood descendants of Adam and Eve emigrated from the two centers of violet culture.

These superior pioneers bravely forfeited the comforts and security of the Adamic centers to join with humans, where they lived, to create hybrid populations destined to advance civilization. Those men and women became the living impetus to explore the world, eventually taking some measure of Adamic culture, ideals, and physique to diverse and distant lands.

The tall, robust, and attractive violet-skinned children of Eve and Adam were a sight to behold. But along with their stunning physical attributes, the people of their day noticed the ability of the Adamic races to better discern, live, and teach spiritual truths. The superhuman inheritance bestowed on the human race by the Adamites created a more spiritually receptive offspring, another signal goal of the Gardens of Eden and Adamic culture.

Often the children raised in the Garden became priests, teachers, and doctors before venturing out, as with the sons of Seth whose teachings eventually spanned the world. Seth's son, Enos, expanded Seth's work significantly by simply commissioning more and better teachers, well-trained in Adamic ideals and culture, some going far afield.

It is no minor task transforming a world of warring savages into a peace-loving sphere of enlightened gardeners. Eve once told Lyla, "On their world of assignment, Adams and Eves sometimes face great difficulties, especially on quarantined worlds. When we arrive on our bestowal world, it may still have thousands of languages and just as many tribal religions. If a Prince has rebelled, the ensuing darkness—the rejection of the divine plan—triggers in the residual animal mind an instinctual resistance to fraternity and harmony, to the doing of the will of the Father. Such ideal traits as brotherliness and cooperation are seen as faults rather than heaven's way."

Van taught that, "When Adams and Eves leave a world after tens of thousands of years, having the help of many celestial agencies, they have transformed the polyglot, clannish tribes led by self-absorbed chieftains into a real civilization rooted in divine values and ready to join the ranks of mature worlds. They are ready to receive the next order of sonship for further enlightenment and greater levels of God-consciousness and cosmic inclusion."

One of the Lylas asked Eve, "What will happen to you and Adam after you resurrect on the mansion worlds?"

She replied, "On an average world, after the Adamic mission is complete, no more will the pair labor on another evolutionary world. Rather do they join the ranks of surviving mortals and ascend with them on the long journey to Paradise.

"Ascenders always move forward in class formations. The entire cosmos is one gigantic school, where all are students, and all are teachers. Wherever we go in a vast universe, we are tenderly cared for by the angels and others who work for the advancement and benefit of all. We are advanced in heaven by the ministry of angels, in much the same way as human parents care for and educate their children on Earth."

Before the original Lyla died, she recorded that Eve, Adam, and their growing family had created a collection of new musical instruments. The ancient drumbeats of natives were added to sounds and harmonies that enthralled every hearer and inspired the creation of even more kinds of music and instruments on which to play them. All Adamic children share the gift of harmony. "Music is the universal language," was a truth taught to the sound artists and music makers of the Gardens. And music ever remains an artistic endeavor, a reach upward for divine melody and celestial harmony.

Other valuable gifts for which the world can thank Adam and Eve are humor and play. Their world-roaming children imbued the natives with this invisible sense of lightness that keeps away the darkness of overly serious self-contemplation. "Anxiety cannot survive laughter," was another maxim of the Garden schools.

When the children of Adam and Eve mated with humans, they and their offspring evinced a heightened curiosity; they explored until every continent was found, until every person, tribe, clan, city, and nation had been touched physically, intellectually, or spiritually. They took with them the pacific ideals of Eden, that peace is better than war, that commerce is the great peace-maker, and that every human is a child of God, worthy of divine dignity. Even so, there will always be those who resist divine ideals. The belligerent tendency of the human race is a mighty tide to turn.

The single greatest contribution Adam and Eve made to the world was to prepare the way for a ministering Son of even higher origin. Thirty-six thousand years after Eve and Adam arrived on Earth, another descending personality visited. That divine personage became the anchor of time, even the Way, the Truth, and the Life.

Adam and Eve taught that our Father always sends instructors and uplifters when his ascending children are ready. The Life Carriers plant their seeds on barren worlds. They germinate, propagate, radiate, and eventually flower as animal forms, then humans. And on the human alone, God bestows his spirit, so that we may commune directly with our creator. But the evolution and development of the capacity to host God's spirit requires periodic assistance from above. Much of it, very much, comes from an order of beings known everywhere simply as Adam and Eve.

Van, before the pair arrived on the Earth, taught this: "Normally, the Adams and Eves come to a world of hunters and leave a world of gardeners. Then, when they finally depart, another descending teacher comes to further enlighten and lift the world."

Adam and Eve's seminal influence eventually spawned a scientific age that challenged and corrected many of our crippling and backwards superstitions. After their visit, science partnered with curiosity and the pursuit of reliable facts. This fostered a growing ability to solve humanity's persistent problems. It is unfortunate, and counter to the Adamic nature, that science has also created the possibility of self-annihilation.

But the most valuable of all things the Adamic pair bequeathed humanity, and perhaps civilization's saving grace, is greater spiritual receptivity, an expanded capacity for revelation. Revelation, they taught, is a regular feature of evolutionary worlds. Also, of inestimable value are insights into cosmic understanding—facts about universe origin, history, and destiny.

The inherent inventiveness of violet culture led to more leisure, providing humans with more time to contemplate and plan life, even eternal life. Humanity requires a certain amount of leisure to cultivate true religion, actual experience with God.

The Lylas recorded that, for thousands of years, the second Garden continued to be the "cradle of civilization." Sons and daughters of the violet people went forth from their beautiful garden home to the far points of the Earth. By this method the violet descendants very gradually amalgamated their heritage with most of humanity's. And we benefitted thereby, in a variety of ways, not the least of which are family love and the enthronement of woman as man's equal partner in destiny.

As to the fate of the physical Gardens, the Lylas after Adam and Eve's times reported the entire peninsula, on which the first Garden sat, slowly sank and gradually disappeared below the water's surface. Some remnants of the second Garden lay buried in the Euphrates valley, including Adam and Eve's bones. Long after their epoch-making lives ended, Garden culture lives on around the world, unknown to most of its beneficiaries.

EPILOGUE

According to the divine plan, when the violet heritage is mixed with the human, equilibrium between the two races is sometime reached. Humanity is greatly advantaged thereby, shaving off eons of otherwise slow evolution. Even though they defaulted, Adam and Eve's short tenure on Earth netted lasting results in intellectual and social achievements. Eventually their bestowal flowered into the worldwide civilization of today; a global culture of expanding ethical and moral understanding, along with myriad work-saving inventions.

Every race within the whole human family has benefited from Eve and Adam's visit almost forty thousand years ago. The emerging science of human genealogy has discovered evidence of a mysterious mutation in our genetic lineage occurring about that time. This unexplained increase in brain physiology marked a profound improvement in human intelligence, creativity, and inventiveness.

Today, the races are so admixed as to make distinctions trivial. But we still possess a marvelous array of Adamic traits that expand the limits of human potential. Our original racial diversity, and the Adamic infusion, ensures the greatest possible range of human experience. Life itself reveals that the cosmos is infinitely diverse, and without replication. Everyone and everything is unique—even "identical" twins have different freckles. Yet, the whole cosmos is composed of but three things: matter, mind, and spirit. These three cosmic constants are expressed philosophically and ideally by the highest conceptions of truth, beauty, and goodness, but they are experienced in life simply as thing, meaning, and value. Such teachings can only be revelation from higher sources.

I am certain Adam and Eve would send loving greetings to the current residents of their former home, if such were permitted. I believe they still watch over the children of the Earth, cheering our every progress, lamenting our failures, and exhorting us to press on to the goal, the dawn of the ages of Light and Life. It is a welcome relief, and a compelling inspiration, to know that one day the whole sphere will become a genuine Garden of God, one of trillions upon trillions of unique spheres that make up the universe of universes.

It's important to know our true origin, to realize and reckon with the totality of Adam and Eve's teachings. There is great need for such knowledge now, the real story of the violet race, of superhuman love and catastrophic failure. Aside from that one failure, the entire population of the world, most of whom have the pair in their genetic lineage, should know they made significant and lasting contributions to the physical, intellectual, and spiritual well-being of global civilization.

Now we can overturn the injustice—the false narrative—that the parents of the violet race burdened all other races with "original sin." Pass this story on so that truth-seekers can discover the hidden history and the significant lessons, inspiring and tragic, that are the legacy of both Gardens of Eden.

Even though Adam and Eve fell into error early on, they still established the greatest human family of all. Almost all of us carry some small percentage of their blood. The best-known Adam and Eve story does tell of a tragedy occurring long ago in a Garden of Eden. Unfortunately, the Biblical record of those events has been grievously distorted. It became an allegory for the struggle between good and evil, featuring a speaking serpent who tricked innocent Eve into committing evil, the tasting of a Garden fruit which God, for some unrevealed reason, forbade.

As with any powerful myth, the seeds of truth are there, even if the facts are not. The story my family kept is much more believable, complex, coherent, and fascinating than the traditional one. And the world is mature enough now to revisit our past, in light of modern scientific understanding and the intelligent use of the divine gift of spiritual insight.

Never should we forget the marvelous gems of insight and enlightenment that Eve and Adam brought. Their lives, notwithstanding that single failure, gave the Earth and other quarantined worlds valuable lessons on several levels. The actual lives of Eve and Adam are relevant to all times and all worlds. They were sent to create a new social order; a paradise on Earth, something humans instinctively crave and know can be achieved. They came to establish advanced global culture, to bear up more souls for God. According to the Adamic teachings, the Earth and planets like it are soul nurseries. The Adamic mission is to make the nurseries better and more productive. They partially succeeded, not unlike most other lives lived on Earth. Fortunately for them and us, divine mercy provides forgiveness in this life, and a way to greater success in the next.

If beings sent from on high have difficulties, stumble, and cause catastrophic defaults, it is no great wonder when we humans fail in our attempts to create a workable utopia. We will never stop trying, rightfully so! But we all too often fail to learn from our mistakes, thereby forsaking vital solutions for complex social, civil, and spiritual problems. Such solutions are the foundation stones of a lasting and worthy civilization.

I know my family's story is very different from accepted pre-history. Nonetheless, always did my forebears affirm their belief that the Gardens of Eden did exist. And we believe the story is not mythical, allegorical, or metaphorical. According to the family's long tradition, arcing back to the first Lyla, the record is literally true. Such a historically profound account ought not be forgotten. And when recalled, its timeless lessons should not be ignored.

The story of Adam and Eve's sojourn on the Earth is remarkable, instructive, and in the second Garden, somewhat triumphal. It reveals knowledge and insight that can correct and clarify the traditional story about Eden, even our origin fables. The traditional myth about their lives has become just a poor and puzzling tale, a blurry shadow of the far more fascinating real-life chronicle of the bestowal of Adam and Eve on the Earth, and what came before and after them.

Any life would be a futile and tragic exercise if it was without meaning, produced no value, and had no worthy purpose. Such a materialistic life could not long exist in God's spirit reality. If the teachings of Adam and Eve are true, a divinely ordered society can and will evolve on Earth. But only after the sons and daughters of the Earth harmonize with the sons and daughters of God who never cease descending from heaven above, not until they have created a heaven below. Someday, long into the future, under the visible leadership of another descending representative of God, the Earth will become a perfected sphere, a unique Garden floating in time and space, endlessly producing spiritual fruit for God, even our souls.

***

Author's note: *The Gardens of Eden, Life and Times of Adam and Eve* is based on Papers 73-76 of *The Urantia Book*. Free downloads of *The Urantia Book* in the major languages are available at: urantia.org

Printed in Great Britain
by Amazon

32072798R00109